# Mixed Emotions

# (MIS)TAKEN

# KATY HUNTER

(Mis)Taken
ISBN # 978-1-80250-964-9
©Copyright Katy Hunter 2022
Cover Art by Erin Dameron-Hill ©Copyright July 2022
Interior text design by Claire Siemaszkiewicz
Totally Bound Publishing

# (MIS)TAKEN

# Dedication

This one is for Vic and Rob. Two of the bestest friends I could have wished for.

# Chapter One

*The day before*
*Penny*

*Penny, you're a strong, capable woman. You will not falter at the sight of an exposed ab, a kissable lip or a murmured 'I love you'. You've got this. You can do it.*

I raise a trembling hand to knock, hesitating before going in for the kill.

To be entirely truthful, I don't have 'it' at all. In fact, I'm about as far from having 'it' as a person can be, but Kelli's eyes are burning a hole in my back as she stares me down from her car—willing me to do the right thing—and I don't want to get my proverbial arse kicked if I fuck this up.

To my surprise, the front door opens. The decision is made for me. "Hey, Penny."

"Hey." Reece's stunning older sister Chloe brushes past me, giving me a quick peck on the cheek and leaving the door wide open. Her manner is such that I'm pretty sure she has no idea why I'm here or what her brother has been up to. This doesn't shock me. The man is sly. He's not going to let the world — or his family — know that he fucked up another relationship.

"Reeeece, Penny's here," she yells over her shoulder as she leaves.

Would he have answered if he hadn't been forced to? It's been two weeks and the man has completely ignored my calls and been suspiciously absent every time I come by. *The Art of Ghosting* by Reece Sheffield. It wouldn't sell well, the proof being that I'm standing on his doorstep right now listening to him come down the stairs.

A conversation is well overdue, and now he can't avoid it. *Good.* At least it'll be over with.

He saunters down the corridor. Reece's at-home attire is a pair of gray tracksuit bottoms. He's been wearing them for so long that the crotch has started to thin and the elastic in the waist has gone to shit. He never wears anything underneath them, so I — and possibly all his neighbors — am treated to more than just an impression of his family jewels.

He scratches the back of his neck then rubs it. Too much late-night gaming again. Not my problem anymore.

Then he slips his hand into his pocket and scratches his junk.

*Don't look at his penis.* I allow my eyes to drop down, just for a second. I can see why Kelli felt like I needed back-up for this mission. I am confoundedly drawn to the enemy.

He has bags under his eyes and the imprint of his pillow on his cheek, but he's still devastatingly handsome. Even his hair is flattened on one side, which should be wholly unattractive and yet, *God…* I want to run my fingers through it, pull at it, hold it while he…

Kelli's voice seeps into my mind. *"Don't fall for him again. I'm warning you. I won't be afraid to get out of this car and tell him exactly what I think of him. It won't be pretty, Pen."*

"Hey," he says, flashing me a subtle smile and leaning into the doorway. "You want to come in?"

*Yes, please. Damn it. No. Be strong. Ignore the dimples. Move away from those come-to-bed eyes.*

"Nah. I'll just make this quick, shall I? It's over. As if it could be anything else after what you've done. I'll get someone to drop your stuff off, and if you could do the same, then we can close the Chapter on this whole thing."

"Pen…" He takes his hand out of his pocket and scratches his abs, revealing just a glimpse of the little hairline that runs up his stomach. I used to kiss that, on my way down. That might be the bit of him I'll miss the most. "Don't be like that."

*"Don't be like that?" What the fuck?* Tomorrow was supposed to have been our wedding day.

"We haven't spoken in two weeks. We were getting married, buying a flat, growing old together. Remember that?"

"Yeah…" He contorts his face into the most unpleasant grimace, like I've just suggested that he clean the skid marks off the toilet. "No. I can't do that anymore."

He's so casual, almost emotionless…as if he's canceling a lunch date.

"I figured that when you ran away the other day, *during sex*, and haven't spoken to me since."

It had been *terrible* sex. Neither of us had been in the mood. We'd been arguing the finer details of our quickie registry office wedding, and all I'd wanted was the final say on the flowers. I *may* have asked him about petunias as he pounded away aimlessly. It wasn't my finest moment, and if it's any consolation, I do regret it, but still, I'm not sure it quite merited *this*.

"Yeah." I've never noticed how monosyllabic he is until now. "Sorry."

I cackle. "Sorry? Are you sorry for cheating, too?"

This one throws him. When he isn't half-asleep in his manky old clothes, Reece is on everybody's TV from nine a.m. until lunchtime. Suited and booted, he climbs into a company car every day—an air of complete confidence—and heads off to convince everybody that he is the perfect gent. Witty, handsome, caring... He has the whole country fooled into thinking he's such a fucking catch. That was the man I'd fallen in love with, and that is the man who is about to emerge onto the doorstep at the realization that *I* am dumping *him*.

This isn't me begging him to come back. This is me telling him he can fuck right off. From the look of the storm brewing in his eyes, he is *not* happy about it.

He narrows his eyes. "I didn't cheat on you, Pen. I walked out on you two weeks ago and found myself someone who wasn't so desperate to get married and have babies and all that shit—someone who pays attention when I'm fucking her."

"We were *engaged*, Reece. Nobody forced you into proposing."

"You haven't talked about anything else since you met me. You keep bridal magazines on your coffee table. You decided where we were going to live, our kids' names and you even chose a fucking puppy at the shelter." I step back. His voice has a tinge of menace, and confrontation isn't my thing. I wouldn't have come here today, but Kelli made me.

"*That's what best friends are for,*" she'd said as she'd dropped me off at the end of the road. "*Now go dump that idiot.*"

She has never liked the man. Now I'm starting to come across to her point of view. What had I been thinking? Perhaps, more specifically, which part of my body had I been thinking with? The man is a dream. Even a grungy T-shirt and skanky old trousers can't hide that.

Reece unfurls his hand from his neck and places it on my reddened cheek, pulling me closer. "You're angry with me. I get it. I *am* sorry." He leans in closer. "You sure you don't want to come in and let me make it up to you? One last time."

He smells like sleep and sweat and the aftershave I bought him for Christmas — and familiarity. I close my eyes, exulting in that delicious scent.

How amazing it used to feel when he held me so tightly that I thought he'd never let go.

How loved I was.

He brushes his lips against mine and a car horn honks loudly, making us both jump. Reece looks over my shoulder, trying to see who's out there.

"I can't do this. It's over." I hold out my hand. "Here's the ring. Thanks for the memories. Enjoy your incredible new girlfriend who doesn't mind the fact that nine times out of ten you're too tired for foreplay." Reece being 'not really into' going down on me had been somewhat of a relief. The man was terrible at it. He thinks the clit is to be treated like a button on a PlayStation handset, flicked relentlessly. He doesn't do subtle. He does quick and to the point. If lady-parts could curl up in horror, I'm pretty sure mine had just done that at the thought of being in this man's hands again.

He pushes my palm away, the ring still in it. "You won't find anyone like me."

*I fucking hope not.*

"I have options. So many options," I reply, with an air of self-confidence that's fooling nobody. I don't have a single option...not one. He leans his head to one side, contemplating the fact that somebody might be interested in me. My phone rings. 'Cute Coffee Shop Guy' is calling me, apparently. "Hello?"

Before I can stop him, Reece leans forward and puts the call on speaker. *What the fuck?*

"Hey, Penny, it's Jake. We met at the coffee shop the other day. You gave me your number for a gig."

"Hi, Jake." I know that voice, but can't quite place it. "What can I do for you?" Reece steps back into the door-well. I lift a hand, as if to wave goodbye, and back away a couple of feet.

"Look. I know you said you have a boyfriend, but, fuck it, I just wanted to say that if you're ever free..."

I glance back up at Reece, shrug my shoulders and smile. "I'm free tonight."

"You are?"

"Sure. Hold on a second. I'll just finish what I'm doing, and we'll work out the details." I stroll back over to a shocked Reece, lean in and peck him on the cheek. "So. Many. Options."

I lift the phone to my ear and chat away as I walk back down the street to Kelli's car, not even bothering to take him off speaker. This is a glorious moment and I want everybody to enjoy it, Reece especially.

I also slide the very expensive diamond ring back onto my finger. *Hell, I deserve it.* I washed that man's dirty underwear while he was sleeping with someone else. I should have married him *then* left his sorry arse.

"You killed it," she cries, hugging me as I slide into the passenger seat. "I knew you could do it."

I point at the phone. "*Jake*? Really? I thought Reece was going to twig."

She winks at me. "What is the point of me having the most *adorable* cousins if I can't use them to get back at that cheating dickhead of an ex-fiancé of yours?"

I grin. "True. Did you see his face? Oh my God. And I almost kissed him. Ugh. I'm so pathetic."

"You are," she replies, starting up the engine. "But I love you anyway. Now, how about we stock up on tequila and ice cream. In a couple of hours, you're going to remember that tomorrow was supposed to be your wedding day and you're going to be a mess."

"I'm fine." I'm on a high. Nothing can top the look on that man's face and the way I'm feeling right now. Kelli purses her lips. She knows me far too well. I'll be a sobbing wreck in a couple of hours and only margaritas can heal that type of pain.

\* \* \* \*

Kelli hands me a cocktail, which is deceptively orange, considering it's ninety-five percent alcohol. "He's a dick."

"No, it's my fault. I did it again."

"You did nothing wrong." She takes my hand. "Nobody forced him to put that ring on your finger."

"True." But I'd been sowing the seeds since we'd met. Marriage, babies, a home, that's the goal. That's always the goal and always the problem. Sometimes I let that goal spill out from my internal thoughts to my external ones. "I think I gaslighted him into proposing. I'm very persuasive."

"Fuck off. You should have given him a kick where it hurts. What a tosser, running off mid-sex. I can't believe it." She downs her cocktail, inciting me to do the same, then pours us another. "I mean, who makes someone move to another city, proposes to them then just fucks off, you know, while they're fucking. *Fucker*." Kelli is not one to mince her words.

"Can we change the subject?" I'd rather talk about anything than that man. I can't stop thinking about that hand running across those abs and how I'll never see or touch them again. I was right. I *will* miss that delicious line of hair the most.

"We sure can. You know what this night needs?" She pulls out a folder from under the coffee table, but it's not just any folder. It's a big pink four-clip wedding file covered in cut-out pictures from old teen magazines. "Perfect Husband Dan Scott."

*Oh my God.* I can't believe she kept that thing. We must have made it when we were fourteen. "Not Fucking Perfect Husband Dan Scott."

"Perfect Husband Dan wouldn't pull out and run. He'd smother the bed in rose petals then he'd smother your body with his until you couldn't take it anymore."

I grab the folder, open it to a random page. "True. And puppies... He'd get me a puppy. No, two puppies. No, he'd adopt *all* the puppies from the shelter."

"Yeah, he would. That's more like it. Then he'd invite you back to his beach house for romantic walks on the sand at sunset." *Oh, the dream.* Holding hands as we stroll along the beach. No need for words, as we know we love each other with a glance and a smile.

"Exactly. Yes. Can I have another one of your delicious cocktails?" Kelli serves me another drink and I turn the page. A photo from some random wedding shoot Dan did for a movie with my head glued on in the place of the bride stares back at me. It's like something out of a serial killer's lair. "Fuck, that's a bit warped."

Kelli peeps over my shoulder "Yeah, I think we went too far with that one."

Before it made it into the folder, that picture used to be on my wall. Before I even knew Dan, he was by my side being the perfect husband, waiting for me to grow up and marry him for real.

Dan might not really be the man of my dreams—that's just a joke that Kelli likes to perpetuate—but I love him very much. In fact, not a week goes by that I don't send him a 'Hi, how are you doing?' via our secret little WhatsApp group. He always replies something rock-and-roll like 'wasted' or 'chilling'. It's our thing and we've done it for five years now without a single person knowing about it.

He's more Secret Best Friend Dan Scott, but she doesn't need to know about that. I keep that for me.

The souvenirs that Kelli and I created to distract us from the torn shreds of our lives are just a silly game, but that folder reminds me of the actual dream—the one I keep in my heart, the one where I fall in love forever.

Perfect Husband *Somebody* has to exist, doesn't he?

# Chapter Two

*Day One*
*Pace*

"Pacey James Scott." Mom stands on the other side of the hotel room door, acting like she hasn't been hanging around for the last twenty minutes waiting for one of us to emerge.

"Yes, Mother?"

"Where is your brother?" Mom is pissed and somehow it's my fault, again. I turn to look. Dan is lying on my bed in only his boxers, scrolling through his messages and avoiding our dearest mother. He shushes me and does the international hand sway across the neck signal for 'get rid of her'.

"He's on my bed, Mom." I throw him my "evil twin' smile and carry on with my packing.

We've been in the UK a week, and in that time, I've seen him maybe once. Dan the superstar has way more important things to do than watching the Trooping of the Color with his family, and let's face it, ninety-nine percent of those things involved being naked in a bed with a variety of people — at the same time, of course.

My mother storms into the room, her finger pointed, ready for war. "Dan Everett Scott, are you avoiding me?"

Dan has two options at this point. Pretend he's asleep or play the innocent son. Considering that he's snuggled up with what looks suspiciously like a very young Jack Russell puppy — both of them looking like butter wouldn't melt — he opts for the former.

Stretching out his arms, then rubbing his eyes, he points at the dog. "Mom, you'll wake the baby."

She melts, as she always does when it comes to her favorite son, and calms down a notch or two, even if, from the sneer on her face, she's not so sure about the dog. "He's cute but he shouldn't be on the bed. Whose puppy is he?"

"This is Gus. My…uh…my fiancée's dog."

I've no idea where that dog came from or how he ended up in my bed, but there's one thing I know for sure and that's that this dog does not belong to Dan's fiancée — for the simple reason that that woman doesn't even exist.

"Well, isn't he just darling? Can he travel? Has she had him vaccinated and all that?"

"Mm-hmm." Dan's eyes widen. This hadn't even occurred to him until the moment Mom mentioned it. He reaches down onto the floor and ruffles around in a bag. "Yup, passport, vaccinations. We're all good." Wherever this dog came from, it looks like we're keeping it. This is not just something he picked up on the street on the way home. Somebody *gave* this dog to my brother, most likely in the hope that it would lead to a relationship in some way.

*Damn it*, have people not met Dan? He can barely shower on a daily basis. What the hell is he going to do with a dog?

I look at that cute little face, that poor pupper about to be unleashed into a life of being handed from PA to dogwalker and back again.

I guess I own a dog now.

"Talking of your lovely fiancée, where is she? Is she on her way?"

I bite my lip and the grin on my face grows into the widest smile. Dan, the golden boy, the one who can never do anything wrong, has royally fucked up, and it feels *so* good to be here to see it.

When an online source claimed that he'd been entertaining a harem of women, Mom went ballistic. We don't do *ménage à trois* — or *quatre* or *cinq* — in our family. We do relationships and marriage and settling down.

I should know. I have failed spectacularly to find myself a girlfriend who wants to stick with me longer than five minutes. The constant reminder from my mom — quite often in front of any woman I dare to introduce her to — that *my* love life is probably more of a disappointment to her than it is to me doesn't help with finding 'the one'.

But anyway, back to my brother's fuck-ups. He came up with a winning idea. Create a girlfriend. No, even better, a fiancée. Only problem was that the dickhead didn't actually think to find himself a suitable girl for the role. Let's just say that anyone he'd choose to bring home would not be Mom's cup of tea.

And the lie is coming to fruition. Fake fiancée is supposed to be coming with us to Dan's place in Spain. Today. In less than an hour.

"I know you want to keep it a surprise, but can you at least tell me her name?" Dan picks up his phone, scrolls through it, as if that is going to make Mom go away. "Daniel, I'm talking to you."

"Uhh…Penny."

"Penny?" says Mom. "Why does that name sound so familiar?"

"Most popular brand of inflatable doll?" I murmur under my breath.

"Hey, that's my girlfriend you're talking about," says Dan, looking about as affronted as one can when your twin brother has just insulted someone who doesn't even exist. "A little respect."

Mom, who has chosen to ignore our shenanigans, gleams with joy at the idea of her prodigal son bringing home his future wife. *Oh boy. This is going to be awesome.*

I give him the finger from behind Mom. "Pace, I can see you, you know," she says. *How?*

"She's meeting us at the airport," says Dan. "Now, please, can you all just go so I can get showered and dressed?"

"This is my room, dude."

He looks down at the dog and back at me. "Oh yeah. Did I sleep here last night?" Yes, bro, yes, you did. You came into my room hammered at three a.m. and slid into bed next to me, handed me a puppy, farted then snored until six.

For fuck's sake, why did I ever agree to this? A month. A whole fucking month with these two and Dad — who never moves from his armchair, except to get the paper — and our darling little sister Emma. Her only goal in life, since about two months ago, is to be a TikTok influencer. I've still got the bruises on my arm from the flight over. Eight hours of being elbowed by her as she practiced her 'moves'.

*Ugh*. Family.

# Chapter Three

*Penny*

We trundle through the crowd, weaving our way past screaming children and the really annoying people who stop dead in their tracks to look at the arrivals and departures boards.

Maybe fewer cocktails last night would have been a good idea. My head feels like someone is currently hammering a hundred nails into it. I love Kelli and her 'getting-over-your-fiancé' parties, but the morning after is always so hard, especially when you have to get up at the ungodly hour of six a.m. She's never bothered. That woman always looks fantastic, whatever the time of day, however she feels. I'm almost embarrassed to be standing next to her.

I don't normally see mornings. My job takes me into the early hours, then I get home and eat and watch TV. I guess I have seen six a.m. once or twice as I'm closing the curtains and heading off to bed.

I didn't bring my mixing table or any of my gear, and I'm regretting it now. I'm going to be stuck in that beautiful apartment for two whole weeks with Kelli, who is going to insist we hit the clubs and bars every night for three days then she's going to spend the next week and a half sleeping it off on the beach or in somebody else's bed. Kelli doesn't do falling in love or 'any of that nonsense', as she calls it. She has adventures and affairs.

I was planning to make some beautiful music from my heartbreak. DJs can be tortured souls. We're artists, too, creating magical melodies to stir your soul. *I should write that down and put it on a T-shirt.*

The only thing I'm creating at the precise moment, though, is a desperate thirst and, at the same time, a deep desire to empty my guts.

We drop off our bags and head through security. Reece had insisted on first-class tickets for our honeymoon. I don't really do first-class as a rule, but he paid, and I am not wasting the opportunity to get every last penny out of the man who should have been marrying me today. Petty revenge feels so good, despite my pounding headache. At some point in the early hours, it was decided that Kelli would come, too. We went onto the website, booked earlier flights and transferred the ticket over to Kelli's name. Then I changed Reece's password, just in case he suddenly remembered he'd paid for the honeymoon and wanted to cancel. I feel like that was a magnificent achievement, considering the amount of alcohol that had been consumed by that point.

Kelli's excuse for coming with me was that I can't be trusted not to fall in love with the first man I see. *Ridiculous.* Okay, not ridiculous, but unlikely. Okay, she probably has a point, but I'm a romantic. Falling in love is what I do best. It's the aftermath that's the problem.

We head for the executive lounge, where I'm contemplating some hair of the dog. A mimosa's virtually a fruit anyway, isn't it? "I need a drink."

"You need water."

"I'm on holiday, I'm heartbroken and I deserve it."

I assumed my attire would warrant at the very least a second glance from the man at reception, but he checks our tickets and ushers us through as if everybody in first-class wears neon cropped tops and khaki cargo pants.

"Late nineties, early two-thousands is totally in," Kelli insists as I tug at my top, trying to cover up my bloated belly.

This morning she'd rifled through my suitcase, thrown my clothes out and replaced them with crop tops and cute short shorts before driving me to the airport. For several years now she has officially been my stylist when it comes to formal events. I love her, but that woman is fashion and I am not. Taking me out of my comfort zone brings that girl so much joy, but honestly, I just don't do exposed flesh. I like my baggy T-shirts and mom jeans. She likes me to look like I just stepped off a runway. I sneaked a few T-shirts back in when she wasn't looking. Can't go on holiday without my favorite concert tee collection.

She put dresses in there, too. Seriously? Wafty, flowery summer dresses and sleek, sexy numbers. Does she not know me at all?

I place a hand over my growling stomach. My pasty abs haven't seen the light of day for years. Heartbroken-and-hungover me is not in the mood to make fashion statements.

We walk down a long corridor and through to the lounge. Water bottles by the million adorn a side bar. I grab one and offer another to Kelli.

"No, thanks. I have to wee. Do we have time?"

"Go. I'll find us somewhere to sit. We've got loads of time, so no stress." I go off in search of a comfy seat with a view of the planes.

I don't want to make conversation, so I skip the first couple of seating areas—where there are people who look like they might entertain the idea of small talk—and keep walking. I plan to read on holiday. I've got a handful of romance novels and a heart that needs mending. Some good old-fashioned happy-ever-afters are what this girl needs.

A loud group blocks my route and I struggle to go around or past them. It's made up of eight or so noisy Americans with their backs to me all talking at once—and what looks suspiciously like a puppy. *Who brings a dog onto a plane?*

They don't seem to want to move out of the way, so I just stand there rolling my eyes and sighing loudly as they decide what to do. I'm English. Passive-aggressive silent complaining is what we do best.

At the back of the group, a glamorous older lady turns away for a second, sneezes into her elbow and consequently drops the entire contents of her designer shoulder bag onto my feet.

They don't even notice this poor woman—or if they do, they're ignoring her. They're all too busy trying to talk over each other or staring at their phones. The group shuffles forward and she gets more and more annoyed as she tries to bend down to pick it all up in time to catch up with them. Stepping back, I crouch down and hand the items to her one by one.

"Thank you," she says as I pass her a Chapstick and a set of keys.

"No problem," I reply with a smile. The bending is making me dizzy, but I can't stop now. I'm hardly going to walk away, even if my weary body is not feeling very charitable currently.

"Here you go." She hands me a ten-dollar bill, peering down her nose at me as she does it. I don't quite know how to react, as I can't exactly spend it here or where I'm going, and I didn't expect to be tipped, anyway. She points to the canvas messenger bag slung over my shoulder. I use it to carry my laptop. That thing never leaves my side. It has my whole world in it. "I should get myself one like that. Much more practical," she adds, with a cackling laugh, as if it's the most hilarious thing she has heard all year. *Bitch.*

"Yes." I don't have enough brain cells this morning for a witty retort, so I hand her back her ten-dollar bill, with a polite 'no, thank you' and wait for her to rejoin the group and for them to move out of the bloody way.

I take in their faces as I wait, and my heart literally drops out of my body. I might still be drunk from last night, but I appear to be standing in front of not one but two Dan Scotts. Is that even possible? *Of course, the evil twin.* The way Dan had described him, I'd imagined a scrawny nerd. He's basically a Dan clone with glasses—not scrawny, very un-nerdlike. *Not bad. Not bad at all.*

That said, I've known Dan for five years, so his brother's had a bit of growing time since he'd first described him to me.

*Am I staring? I'm staring, aren't I?*

I sink my hand almost subconsciously to my phone, nestled in one of the millions of pockets in my trousers. I still have a Google alert set for Dan. It's not like it's going to go off because I'm standing so close to him, though, is it? That's not how that works.

*Oh God.* Am I panicking? Can they tell how stressed out I am right now? It's only Dan, for fuck's sake...and his entire family. *Eek.*

The woman glares at me as I freeze, transfixed by the faces of the two men in front of me, "This girl —"

"Dan," I say. I'm still mesmerized by the not-so-evil twin brother — the same piercing green eyes as Dan, the same gorgeous face, but that hair, *oh my.* Dan shaves his curls off then gels them down when they get too long, but this guy lets it just flop over his forehead in the most natural, uncontrolled way. It is mightily hypnotic. I've never *ever* considered myself to have a type — you couldn't put my exes into a line-up and get confused between any of them — but this guy? *Wow.*

"No, I'm Pace," says the god of all that is beautiful, pushing his glasses up his nose and sneering at me, clearly unamused by my apparent mistake. "And I'm betting your name's not Dan, either." I come out of my stupor. Maybe he's not *that* attractive after all.

"Penny," says Dan softly, as his face forms the biggest grin. Every time I bump into him, he's so enchanted to see me. My heart beats a little faster for my old friend Dan.

A collective gasp comes from the group, and the older lady puts a hand on my back and pushes me into the fold.

"Penny. Oh my word. I was not expecting... Oh my. I'm so sorry. Dan didn't even show me a photo of you, and here I am treating you like a complete stranger when you're family." Well, she's changed her tune.

The only person more surprised than me by the situation is Dan's brother, who is looking around as if he's waiting for someone to pop up from behind one of the plush leather seats here and yell, 'Pranked!'

"Penny," repeats Dan, still clearly in shock at seeing me here, "you're here."

I nod, wanting to reply, but my mouth appears to be broken. I'm still reeling from my hangover and seeing him again. Now I'm *family*? *What the fuck is going on?*

"Yes," I reply, with a heartfelt smile. "It's definitely me."

Dan steps forward and pulls me into the tightest hug. I reciprocate. It's Dan, for fuck's sake. *My* Dan.

Of course he's not actually *mine*. He never was. We have one of those special-connection friendships that people have sometimes, like the best friend from school who shared a dislike for biology lessons and a love of skipping class to go off and have adventures. It's the kind of friendship that stays with you — bonded for life.

People always assume we dated, but it was never like that. They don't need to know our business or even how we know each other. It's *complicated*. Sometimes there are things that you don't want to just share with anybody, and that's what it's like for us — keeping our private lives private. I just let them think what they want. Dan's my friend, I love him to bits and that's all they need to know.

He lets go so that both of us can breathe and grabs one of the people from the group, steering me gently away from everybody else. "Karl, did you do this?" The small hipster-looking man, in a very loud suit, shakes his head.

Kelli arrives and pushes in to hear what we're saying.

Dan turns to me, confusion in his eyes. "Who sent you? Why are you here?"

I shake my head. He's inches away from my face and his breath smells like beer and cigarettes.

Bile rises in my chest. I lean away from him, but his hand is still on the small of my back. My hangover, combined with his strong 'life-is-one-long-party' smell, does not make for the best situation. "No. I helped the lady, and I'm just waiting for my flight."

"You're not… Nobody sent you?" He lifts a hand to his chin, scratches the day-old stubble on his face and looks straight into my eyes. "This is just a coincidence?"

"Uh-huh."

He pauses, like he's trying to make sense of it all. "You look…fantastic."

"Thank you. So do you." We both look rough as fuck, but I know exactly what he means.

"She's the DJ," says Karl. "The one from… Uh…" He scrolls down his phone, holds up a photo of me and Reece. "She's been trending all morning."

"What?" Kelli grabs his phone and scrolls down the article. "That utter cockwomble… Listen to this. '*Reece Sheffield, everybody's favorite morning TV host, is reeling from the news that his fiancée, Penny Farthing, otherwise known as DJ NYB, set to pierce the music industry this year, left him on their wedding day for a mysterious lover.*'"

The nausea swirling around my stomach turns to rage.

*I'm going to kill him. I'm going to go back to his house and wipe that grin off his beautiful, smug face.*

"Fuck… You fucking bast…" I catch the older woman's annoyed face glaring at me out of the corner of my eye and clamp my mouth shut. "Sorry."

I'm assuming she's their mum. Dan used to say she looked like she'd had a very sour lemon stuck in her mouth since childbirth, and she fits that description perfectly.

"Whoa," says Dan, scrolling through his own phone. "That guy is pissed. He totally canceled you." He holds it up. Karl was right. I'm trending—and not in a good way. The things people are saying are not nice…not at all. Do their mothers even know that they use that kind of language?

I cover my mouth with my hand in utter shock at some of the comments. "Fuck." I'm not exactly shy of a swearword myself but never online and never aimed at somebody I don't even know.

He pulls me into his arms again. The man just can't stop hugging me. Then he turns away from me, mutters something to Karl, who waves his hands, clearly opposed to whatever he's suggesting.

He turns back to me. "Are you up for some revenge?" I look up at him, still reeling from the slaps that life is throwing at me from every direction. "Well?"

Now, I love Dan with all my heart, but I really don't think I'm in an emotional place to start plotting revenge. As it is, I'm taking my best friend on holiday at my ex's expense, and what more could I do to get back at Reece?

"Absolutely. What do you have in mind?" asks Kelli, fluttering her eyelashes at Dan. She's clearly not bothered by the smell of three-day-old sweat that is emanating from this man. He looks over at her as if he's just noticed she's there, and his eyes light up. *Oh good God*, that man cannot resist *anybody*…except me.

I turn to look at her. "Are you fucking kidding? What are you thinking?"

"Perfect Husband Dan Scott," she says, winking at him. "It's a sign I tell you, *a sign!*" Kelli believes in horoscopes and fortune-tellers and all of that. I do love me some destiny and fate, but this girl is going to be telling me any minute that her runes predicted this very thing. "It's in the stars." Damn. I forgot the stars. They're constantly throwing things our way — like burning meteors and such.

He pulls Karl aside again, whispers for a good couple of minutes, turns back to me, gives me a final lung-emptying hug and strolls back over toward his family.

"Mr. Scott wishes to make you a deal," says Karl, twiddling his bow tie. He gets out his phone and starts writing something down.

"A what?"

"A deal." He adjusts his glasses and lets out a deep, soulful sigh. "I'm to ask you if you and your friend here wouldn't mind spending one week — seven days — with Mr. Scott and his family at their residence in Gran Ventura. You are to be a guest of Mr. Scott, in the guise of his…uh…fiancée, and will act as such in the presence of his parents and siblings. I should add, Miss…uh…Farthing, that you are free to say no to this agreement, walk away and pretend this never happened." He stares at me over his thick-rimmed hipster glasses as if this is clearly the logical thing I should be doing, walking away and not even considering this whole ridiculous affair.

I open my mouth to speak, but nothing comes out. His fiancée? That's ironic.

"A fake girlfriend? With a contract?" says Kelli. She gazes over my shoulder at the aforementioned Mr. Scott and sighs the deepest sigh.

"Kelli, no, I don't think — "

"But he's so damned hot. Famous hot. That's so much hotter than normal hot," she replies, still staring at him like a lion about to pounce on its prey. *God*, woman, get a grip. "And Reece would just die. A total fucking massacre. It's perfect."

Karl points at her as if she has just had the best idea on the planet. "Yes. Yes, exactly. A contract. I think my friend Gary has even done one of those before. There'll need to be something drawn up. You'll need to be reimbursed for your trouble." Kelli raises her eyebrows at me as if to say, 'yay, money!' while Karl scrolls his phone, calls someone then looks back up at me. "No sex, Gary says. Kisses initiated by you, if you wish to do so."

*He's going to need to brush his teeth first. Oh shit, and so will I.*

I breathe into my hand and sniff it. Karl cringes. I'm not making the best first impression. The resulting smell is less than satisfactory.

I lean slightly farther away from him. "Okay."

I mean, why the fuck not? What's the worst that could happen?

Karl rolls his eyes at me like he's lost any shred of respect that he might have held for me up to this point. He pulls the phone away from his ear, holds it to his chest and insists, "You're sure?"

I giggle and tap him on the shoulder. "Honestly, you might not believe me, but this is actually the most positive thing that's happened to me this week."

He looks me up and down and scrunches his nose. "Oh, I believe you, honey. I believe you."

\* \* \* \*

*Pace*

It's all very strange.

"A contract? Are you fucking kidding me?" I say it through my teeth. The jet isn't quite big enough for my mother not to listen in to our conversation. Luckily she's taken the dog off to find a bowl of water. The way she's coddling it, you'd think Dan had finally given her the grandchild she has always insisted we provide.

My brother looks up from his phone, ruffles his greasy hair and winks at me. "What? This solves everything. She stays a week, we catch up, hang out. It's Penny. It's *fine*." He grins as if I know exactly what he's talking about. He leans toward me, away from her and her friend. It's not like he has to worry about them hearing us. They're leaning on each other, their heads back, mouths open, softly snoring and fast asleep. They've been like that since take-off. "Plus, that Kelli girl is *fire*."

"And you don't find that weird? You say Penny's name, and she just appears in the airport." He fidgets and looks away, guiltily. Where did that name come from? It's not as if you meet a girl called Penny every day. "Well?"

He lifts his gaze to mine and grins, falling back into his nonchalant, I-don't-give-a-fuck persona — the one he used to only reserve for everybody else. "Fate. The good Lord loves me."

"If anybody is controlling your fate, bro, it's not coming from up there. You sold your soul years ago."

He chuckles. "True."

I shift in my seat. "What do we know about her? Man, you don't think about these things. You just dive in. She could sell all this to the highest-bidding newspaper."

"Penny is…" He looks over at her with a fondness that I don't think I've ever seen when it comes to my brother and women. He normally wavers between lust and disgust. This is the closest thing to him having feelings since he won that Emmy. He doesn't even look at *me* like that. "Penny is good people."

"What's the story between you two?"

He grabs his phone and hands it to me without answering my question. "This is her website."

DJ NYB. She's had a couple of minor releases, made a name for herself on the club scene in Manchester and Ibiza, but it's nothing to write home about. I glance up at her splayed out in the chair. From the state of her, she likes to party — nothing unusual for someone dating my brother, so that would fit — but she looks like a nice person, someone I would date. Not my brother's type at all.

She seems grounded, down-to-earth — or so I've learned from the little I've spoken to her. Her dark hair, braided to her head like a modern-day Leia, is such a beautiful dark brown. There's no pretentiousness about her. You apparently get what you see.

Now that I think about it, she *does* look a lot like Leia. Maybe she knows the movies. She *has* to. Which one is her favorite? Got to be three to six with that hairstyle. I can just imagine us settling down to watch a sci-fi marathon with a tub of popcorn and a warm blanket over our knees.

*Whoa.* I need to calm my shit. I can already hear Dan's snarky comments in my mind. *"This is why women don't date you, Pace. You've got to stop mentioning* Star Wars." I lean back into my chair and glance around to make sure nobody sees the blush that's burning my cheeks.

I've never looked twice at any woman who is willing to date my brother. It's not like I'm actually considering dating her, right? Plus, she's not real. Well, she's real but she's not really his fiancée. And this is *me* we're talking about.

I just compared this woman to a fictional princess. That's all anybody needs to know about my dating success.

"Ooh, look at them, poor girls. Penny looked really gray this morning." Mom tuts and raises her eyebrows at Dan as she rocks the dog back and forth like a baby. Gus is completely zonked out on her shoulder, loving all the attention. "She's not... You're not..."

"Pregnant? No! Oh my God, Mom. Seriously? Penny worked late. She's a DJ."

She stirs upon hearing her name and wakes with a snort, yelping as she opens her eyes and discovers us all staring at her.

"Hi," she croaks. That woman needs some hydration. She must have been hitting the bottle hard last night. Whatever she's going through, I'm not sure my brother is the cure.

Dan slides a friendly hand into hers, gripping tightly, and she relaxes into it as if they've been together forever.

I swear this plane is taking us into another dimension where my brother is a good person. Dan Scott doesn't hold women's hands. More often than not he'll be found grabbing a butt or a boob, but hands? Nope.

This is just weird.

She smiles at him the way women always do — Dan the handsome movie star with millions upon millions of adoring fans.

I should be flattered. It's my face, too, in many ways. Except — if I'm being honest — they never actually smile at me like that. Dan and I share the same features, but not quite the same charm. I simply begin to speak and the majority of women walk away. I'm not my brother, and I never will be.

And most of the time I'm okay with that, but there's something about Penny — something about her smile, the way she carries herself. I can't explain it. Maybe I've been single so long that I'm finding everybody attractive. Maybe I just want somebody to hold my hand and look into my eyes like she's doing right now to my brother.

I lean back into my chair and contemplate the fact that for the first time in my life I'm coveting my brother's wife.

*Strange indeed it is, young Pacey, Strange indeed it is.*

# Chapter Four

*Penny*

The villa is beautiful. Perched on the edge of the land, a hundred meters from the beach, lording over the boats and gulls and the endless ocean.

Little was said on the shuttle ride from the plane. His family talk over each other all the time — Dan's mother and sister especially — and it was nice to have some peace. He'd whispered into my ear as we'd gotten on the plane, *"Try not to talk until we get some time to get our stories straight."* I'd feigned exhaustion — not difficult after last night — then had actually fallen into a deep, long sleep, enough to take up most of the flight. The bus, however, was trickier. He held my hand and answered for me. It was uncomfortable. I'm not used to being the meek and mild woman, fawning over her big, strong man.

I'd never imagined that I'd find myself holding Dan's hand and snuggling into his shoulder. Sitting next to him on that bus with his fingers wrapped around mine was utterly surreal. We hug and tap each other on the back like bro dudes. We don't do 'intimate'.

The reality of it all disappointed me somewhat. Perfect Husband Dan Scott is supposed to smell like hope and dreams, but instead he emanates stale tobacco and liquor tinged with sweat. This isn't news to me. I'd just assumed that with a little age came personal grooming and pride in one's appearance.

Kelli's folder and her endless talking about how amazing Dan is had just gotten the tiniest bit of me imagining that he'd actually become this perfect person she'd created. If Dan Scott isn't going to be the one to swoop in and save me one day, am I on my own? Is this it? Am I going to have to adult all by myself?

Kelli sat next to us on the bus and spoke about everything. That woman could talk for a living, if that was a thing. She already has Dan's mum in her pocket. They bonded over that TV show about baking that she's constantly making me watch. As we stepped off the bus, they were deep into a conversation about perfect tips for making your Victoria sponge rise.

I'm quite sure neither of those women has touched a whisk or a mixing bowl in their lives, but who am I to judge?

Dan's brother spent most of the journey playing with the dog. A little birdy whispered in my ear that it's my dog, if anybody asks, and that his name is Gus. I've gained a fiancé and a puppy in the space of a few hours, and frankly it's all a bit much.

My greatest failing, according to the rest of the world, is that I always want to jump right into marriage and babies. Right now, though, the thought of a ready-made family, commitment and all that jazz is slightly overwhelming — probably because under all of my clothes in my suitcase, wrapped up in a plastic bin bag, I've got my wedding dress. I never got to wear it and didn't even get to try it on when it had been delivered. It had been just sitting there waiting to be loved, so I've brought it. I have no idea what I plan to do with it. No good can come of dwelling on the past.

I put my bags down by the bed and wander outside. The upstairs bedrooms all share one long balcony that stretches around the back of the house. I can hear Dan's brother, Pace, cursing out the dog for peeing on something.

Farther down, their mother is doing the same to their father. That poor man hasn't spoken once since I met him. He just sits in a corner, book in hand, ignored by his loud family. I'm pretty sure they'd wear me down, too, if I had to spend a lifetime with them. There's a lot of personality in these people and a truckload of energy. It's exhausting.

Dan is downstairs talking to his team. His personal assistant, Karl, follows him everywhere. He also has a personal chef — who everybody refers to, quite aptly, as 'Chef' — and his stylist, Marcus, who isn't even staying at the house. Dan Scott isn't just a person. He's a whole fucking industry.

I look down at the diamond ring on my finger. I should keep it on. It adds authenticity, but it's another reminder of my failings and disappointment. I'm on my honeymoon without a husband. I look out at the ocean and feel the breeze on my face. This is a pitiful state of affairs for such a lovely place.

Pace tiptoes backward out of his room, turns to see me and almost jumps out of his skin. "It's asleep. It ate my shoe, peed on my suitcase and now it's asleep.

That's not a puppy. It's a monster. Some kind of were-beast."

He's like the anti-Dan—clean living, closely shaven—or at least he was when I'd met him this morning, now it's kind of a lunchtime stubble—and well-dressed. If they didn't share the same face, you wouldn't even know those two were twins.

"Maybe he's a baby wookie?" I reply. *Crap*, I've only been here five minutes and I'm already showing my geek.

His mouth curls into the biggest grin. "Yes, a wookie, exactly." He gets flustered for a second, goes to lean on the balcony, misses it with his elbow then finally ends up awkwardly half leaning, half standing. "Let's hope his nap lasts long enough for us to organize some kind of crate."

Even his voice is different from his brother's. They're like Clark Kent and Superman. Dan is all sexy drawl and hot, tight jeans, and Pace is unsuccessful side-parting—the humidity is making his hair curlier by the second—and glasses and awkward silences. Every time I've spoken to him up until this moment, he's acted like he'd rather be doing anything than spending a minute longer in my presence. Even now, he's got a book in his hand, and he's looking down at it longingly.

"He's cute."

He looks up from the book for a second, pushes up his glasses. "When he's sleeping, yes," he replies with a wry smile. "So you're a DJ, right?"

I lean against the railing and look out at the sea. My job always intrigues. "Yes."

"And what made you do it?" His tone is derisive.

*Wow, rude.* I turn to look him in the eyes. "Become a DJ?"

He shakes his head. "Pretend to be my brother's fiancée. Money? Fame?"

I bite my lip. *Crap.* I thought we were doing a good job up until now. I guess twin brothers can't really hide that kind of thing from each other. They just know.

I take a deep breath and scrunch up my nose before conceding defeat. "Revenge. Friendship." That and the fact that my other best friend has set her sights on getting into Dan's pants before sundown. It would have been rude of me to let them both down, even if it does put me in a rather awkward position.

He tilts his head and pushes his glasses up his nose again—clearly a nervous habit because they are just fine. Then he slowly glides his finger down and taps it against his lips, where it stays for second as he contemplates my reply. Now I know what Lois Lane saw in Clark. *Fuck, that's hot.*

"Interesting," he murmurs.

What's interesting is that I can't stop staring into his eyes. *Pull yourself together, woman. Clark Kent was just Superman in disguise, and you do* not *need to date someone like Dan.*

I turn back to look at the sea before he realizes the effect he's having on me. He's not so different from his brother, after all. He's certainly more charming, if a little brusque…harder to read. Dan's an open book, but Pace is complex.

"Revenge on my ex-fiancé as of yesterday. He canceled my wedding, cheated on me then made everybody think it was my fault."

He raises an eyebrow. "*Your* wedding? You said 'my' and not 'our'."

"I did, didn't I? That probably explains a lot more than I'd like to admit. You're not a psychology major, are you?" I'm really not in the mood for being analyzed right now.

"Med school."

*What the fuck?* "Aren't you supposed to be like twenty-five or something to do that?"

He nods. "Yeah, I finished high school at sixteen. While my brother was gracing everyone's TV and cinema screens, I was busy getting my high-school diploma two years early."

"*Holy shit.* Sorry… Didn't mean to swear. That's so cool. Twenty-one doesn't seem old enough to be at med school. That's really impressive."

"I don't feel old enough, either. It's a lot." He leans in close, and I get a whiff of puppy and pheromones. "I like the sound of revenge. I like it better than thinking you're dating my brother."

*Fuck.* My skin prickles and a shiver runs down my spine. Does he know exactly what he's doing to me? That's what he means, right? That he's glad I'm available.

"Vengeance was the clear course of action."

He chuckles. "I wouldn't like to get on your bad—"

"Honey?" Dan's voice interrupts from inside the bedroom. He strides out through the French windows and over to us, sidling up behind me and placing his hands firmly on my shoulders, giving them a little squeeze. I look up at him and he leans down and pecks me on the forehead. "We need to talk."

"Okay. See you later, Pace."

He smiles and turns away, not even addressing his brother. There's something unfinished between those two—an argument that ended badly or maybe was never even had at all. Their faux brotherly love is easy to spot a mile off. They simply don't like each other.

Once alone in the bedroom, Dan throws himself onto the bed and hands me an iPad. "This is the contract. We're supposed to act like a couple at all times — kissing and stuff. While it'll look like we share the same room, I'm going to be sleeping elsewhere."

"Oh." I don't know why I'm surprised. It's not as if he's my actual boyfriend. "Where? Just in case I need you."

"I've made other arrangements. Don't worry. I've always got my phone on me. Karl put your number in mine. I'll text you so you've got it." The actual concept of the fact that I'm doing this and that I'm doing this with Dan Scott of all people hasn't really sunk in yet. I'm ninety-nine percent sure that I'm still drunk from the previous night and that I'm going to wake up in a couple of hours and realize that this was all a very strange dream.

I sit down next to him, shoving his legs out of the way. The man is a spreader, takes up a whole bed. Perhaps sleeping alone won't be such a bad idea after all. "Won't your family be suspicious?"

"How are they going to know? My parents go to bed way before I do, and it's not like they're going to be interrupting us every morning. We're cute little lovebirds who just got engaged. It'll be fine."

"Oh, okay."

The conversation stalls. So many unsaid words. Should I ask? Should we talk about things or should I let him come to me? I do the latter. We've got a week. It can wait.

I look at him laid out on my bed. Kelli, my closest friend in the world who knows all of my secrets, doesn't know how or why I met Dan. She just knows that he's my friend. She's always assumed that we had this wild sexual affair — at least that's what I let her believe. She knows I won't hear a word said against him.

Perfect Husband Dan Scott is a figment of her imagination, something we created as teens and have perpetuated ever since whenever men disappoint us, which is basically every fucking day.

For some reason, this means that I've always assumed that if he ever saw me again, there would be some kind of attraction. There isn't. I mean, he's hot, there's no denying that the man's got the body of a Greek god, but nothing stirs — not a peek or a whimper from my lady-parts. Dry as a bone.

He is my friend — nothing more, nothing less.

"We can't fuck," he says. I turn to look, as if he's reading my mind. *What now?* "It's written here, in the contract." He points at the screen.

"Okay. Good." I don't know how to respond to that.

"I'm not doing this for that."

"Okay," I repeat, unable to find anything more appropriate to add.

It was never like that, not between us, but it would be nice if he *wanted* to sleep with me. He literally wants to sleep with every other person on the planet.

He sees my pout and throws me a reassuring smile. "And even if we wanted to, because you're so hot and sexy and desirable and all that, the lawyers wouldn't let us."

I raise an eyebrow. "Hot, sexy *and* desirable?"

"Too much?" I nod and punch him in the arm. Dude bros…not lovers.

I'm used to it by now. It's been a week of rejection. One more man to add to the list of men who don't want to sleep with me. I stop playfighting with Dan for a second and look toward the window.

I guess *one* man has found me attractive. That's something, at least.

"So your friend, Katy—"

"Kelli."

He grins. "Yeah. Is she single?"

"Yes, but that doesn't mean you can break her heart." I scooch closer to him. "Do you hear me? Don't you go getting any ideas. She means a lot to me."

Dan leans toward me, his face inches from mine, then he lifts a butt cheek and pulls a joint from his back pocket. "Got it. You want to share?" I shake my head. It was never my thing. He shrugs and gets up off the bed, pointing at the tablet again. "I'm going down to the beach. You need to read the contract and sign it."

"Okay."

He stands up, starts to leave then comes back, bends down, sticks the side of his finger under my chin and gently lifts my face to his. "It's good to see you, pretty Penny. Really good to see you."

Any other person would be a melted puddle of adoration by now, but me? Nothing. Not a single stir in my loins, not a single butterfly. I love Dan Scott with all of my heart but he simply does nothing for me in that way.

He leaves via the balcony. There's a winding staircase at the end of it that leads downstairs. I stay sitting on the bed for a second.

It might be a good time to reevaluate my life plans. Perfect Husband Dan Scott isn't going to marry me one day. He's never going to sweep me off my feet.

That silly little game is over. We can throw away the folder.

I'm on my own.

# Chapter Five

*Pace*

There's a row of bodies on the balcony outside my parents' room. Emma and Mom are stretched out on loungers. Mom is doing a crossword and Emma is doing her best to get along with her. I should be happy for them. I should be overjoyed that my sulky little sister is getting on so well with our ever-so-distant mother, but jealousy bites at me, gnawing away at my confidence.

I tighten my arm around Gus, who is fighting to be put down.

"We're going to the beach. I'm going to take you down to the sea and you can go pee on things down there instead of in my room." He licks my face and pants heavily in my ear. I thought I might find my kindred spirit on my summer trip to Europe, but I wasn't expecting it to be of the canine kind.

He looks up at me with his big, soulful eyes. *Damn it*. He's too cute for words — the only unconditional love I need.

Penny is reading a book — romance, from the look of it. I tilt mine and Gus' heads down and she looks up at us and smiles. I think we're getting on okay. She doesn't know me enough to judge me yet. There's still time for her to be swayed by the rest of them.

She's wearing a Black Sabbath T-shirt over what looks like a very slinky bikini. I shouldn't be looking, but the contrast of one style with another draws the eye. Dan's so fucking lucky he gets to share a room with her every night. She's beautiful. Way, way out of my league.

What even *is* my league? It's been so long since I got the courage up to talk to a woman without dropping something, falling over myself or getting tongue-tied that I don't even know.

Her friend is fast asleep next to her. That woman could turn sleeping into an Olympic sport.

I finally let go of Gus, and he immediately runs into the arms of the enemy.

"How's my baby?" says Mom, crouching down to pet him.

"I'm good," I reply with a smile. Emma rolls her eyes. "Anybody want to come down to the beach with us?"

"Sure," says Emma. "Are you coming, Penny? Mom?" They stretch out their arms, put down their activities and stand. Didn't take long for these guys to get into the relaxed part of the holiday. Kelli doesn't move, and it looks like she's out for the count.

Everyone grabs their towels and other necessities while I chase the little dude along the balcony then we wander down to the sea.

The beach is semi-private. It's shared by all the properties along this stretch. Even if I'm the most successful doctor in my field, I'll never be able to afford something like this. There are four-poster sunbeds and individual loungers. It's a millionaire's paradise.

Dan is already lying out under the sun. He's either high or asleep or both. He's wearing really short, really tight *Baywatch* shorts and is already attracting glances from several women who just happen to be milling around our part of the beach. Gus runs past him then sinks down to bite a mouthful of sand.

"Don't eat it," I shout, pointing my finger at him and trying to catch up. He looks up at me then promptly chomps away.

Penny joins us, laughs at me trying to empty the dog's mouth of sand and hands me a packet of Kleenex from a beach bag the size of a small country. "Oh no. I had a little brother who was a repeat offender at that. He's fifteen now. I think he's probably grown out of it. Did he swallow any?"

"Crap, I hope not. I don't want to spend the rest of my holiday scooping sand out of this guy's mouth and making repeated visits to the vet." I look up at her. "So you come from a big family."

"Six brothers and four sisters. It's…complicated."

"And I thought it was tough with one of each," I reply, throwing her a smile.

She bends down to Gus' level. "Do you want to come for a swim?" He jumps up at her. "You don't mind, do you?" she asks, looking back up at me with a smile.

"No, go ahead. He's supposed to be your dog, anyway, right?"

She cringes. "*Crap.* You're right."

"I'm going to wash the drool-covered sand off my hands. Have fun."

I watch them as they head down to the water's edge, Gus rushing as fast as his little legs will take him.

"She's going to be a great mother," says my mom as she settles down into a lounger with her puzzle book. "She has that maternal instinct." As if she would know anything about that.

I don't know Penny enough to comment. I do know that even if she were marrying Dan, there wouldn't be any kids on the horizon. Mom wants so desperately for him to be 'like everybody else', as she puts it. She believes firmly in the romantic notion that first comes marriage then comes babies. Unfortunately, none of us have done that.

I'm a constant disappointment. Finishing high school two years early didn't even sway her my way. It just caused her even more of a headache. Dan's career had taken off a couple of years before, and she was far too busy living the life of a rich housewife and mother of a famous son to have to deal with sending her other son to college. That's what nannies and drivers were for.

Emma was sent to a private boarding school — that way she didn't get in the way at all. Sometimes I even think she got the better deal. I'd much rather have been alone than have had my mom constantly complaining about my presence.

I sit down in the lounger next to Dan's — my *perfect* brother who believes in polyamory and funky cigarettes. He's probably already got several kids out there. It wouldn't surprise me. An NDA, a hefty check and he moves on to the next woman — or man — or both.

I hate myself for thinking like that. Like, I literally don't care what he does. I just care that it could be the worst thing in the world and my parents would *still* love him more.

"Have you tried therapy?" says Dan as he turns to look at me, lowering his sunglasses and peering over them with his tired, red eyes.

"Huh?"

"Mom speaks to you and you give her your famous nod of agreement and walk away so you don't have to actually have a conversation with her. I know *why*. I just wondered if you'd thought about therapy."

This, coming from my brother who probably lives the most fucked-up existence out of the three of us.

"I walk away so I don't say something I might regret — like the fact that her favorite son and his perfect fiancée are a crock of shit. That's probably something you need to think about. Dealing with — *your* need to constantly please her."

"Oh yeah, no, I agree. The amount of money I spend on therapy because of that woman is eating away into my fortune, but I'm not talking about me. You need to learn to not care."

"We both do." I *shouldn't* care. I should take it for what it is and let it go. I shouldn't feel the need to please my mother, to torture myself like this, wanting so desperately for her to love me like she loves him.

"I'm just saying." He shrugs and his face drops. *Crap.* This is probably the most adult conversation I've had with my brother in a long time, if ever, and I'm dismissing him like it's nothing.

"You're right. It would be better for all of us. Thanks."

He punches me on the arm, just enough to hurt. The international symbol for brotherly love.

\* \* \* \*

*Penny*

Sandy water drips down my T-shirt as Gus' wriggly paws tap against it. Apparently the only way to get this little guy out of the water is to carry him away.

I run up to the loungers where Dan's family are all lined up, soaking up the sun. Kelli has woken up and found her way down to the beach. She's currently sunning herself two loungers down from Dan, and it clearly hasn't escaped his attention that my best friend is to-die-for in a bikini. That woman has a décolleté, and she knows what to do with it.

Pace looks up at me and my soggy little pal. "Oh my God, Penny. You're covered in sand."

He looks terribly concerned, as if it won't ever come off. "It's just an old T-shirt."

"It's a classic." He lifts Gus from my arms. "Thank you."

"No worries."

"You should take that old shirt off, honey. Let us see that lovely bathing suit." Dan's mother has been overly-interested in my clothing and what I should or shouldn't be wearing since I got on the plane this morning. It's a wonder she hasn't been through my wardrobe, deciding what's appropriate for a woman betrothed to her son.

"Oh, I burn really easily, so I like to ease into being in the sun but thank you. It is a lovely bikini. It belongs to Kelli, but she thought it would look amazing on me and she was so right. It does." It's not the first time that people in my life have commented on my individual style, and it won't be the last. I've always found that replying very politely and with way too much information tends to shut people right up. It works a treat on Terri Scott and her desire to see me looking perfect at all times. She huffs and goes back to her crossword.

Pace throws me a sympathetic smile. He looks like he hasn't slept for a week. He also looks like he wants to be anywhere but here. What the hell did his family do to make him hate their presence so much? Admittedly his mom is awful but the rest of them aren't so bad. Certainly not worthy of such disdain.

I'm not one to judge. You never know what's going on behind the scenes.

"Hey, you." Dan jumps up from his lounger, wraps his hands around my waist and snuggles his nose into the crux of my neck. "You smell like the sea."

"I'm going to need a shower after this."

"Mm-m." He peppers me with kisses. "Is that a solo affair or can anyone join in?" *Bloody hell?* Am I missing something or did I suddenly become desirable when I slipped on a bikini?

He winks at me.

*Oh crap. He doesn't mean it. He's acting. My bad.*

I turn my head to face his, pecking him on the nose. "I don't see why not." Play the fiancée. That's what I signed up for. It was supposed to be public, supposed to be revenge, but this is for his family's eyes only—

kind of defeats the object. Reece is never going to see this.

"Get a room," says Kelli, snorting in disgust. What's gotten into her? She was the one who convinced me to do it. She jumps up off of her lounger and storms off, back up to the house.

Dan pecks me on the lips. "Meet me up there." He heads back to the house, too.

God, this is so embarrassing. I would never behave like this in front of my fiancé's family. I catch Pace's eye. He's lost in thought, but his gaze is directly on my breasts as I pat them down.

"Eyes up here," I mutter, and he gasps and catches my glance. His cheeks redden.

"I wasn't. It's… Sorry. They're not… I wasn't."

I throw him a cheeky wink. "Of course not." I look down at my not-very-sizeable boobs. "Why would you?"

"Oh no, I didn't mean… They're perfect. Lovely. Just the right size."

*Seriously?* He gets more and more flustered. "Thank you?"

He opts to just terminate the conversation there, places Gus on the lounger next to him and starts to remove the sand from his paws.

After a few minutes of de-sanding I head off back to the house, too, leaving Pace to shake off the embarrassment. *"Perfect. Lovely."* I've not heard that before. Reece wanted me to get a boob job. I always thought they'd get bigger with pregnancy. It never occurred to me that somebody might like my little breasts just as they were.

A shiver goes down my spine, and I glance back at him.

There's something about Pace. I still can't put my finger on it, but it's becoming more and more evident every time I'm around him.

I don't like the way I feel about him, because the way I feel about him should be reserved for men I want to be with — not just for meaningless sex. I promised Kelli I wouldn't touch a good, settling-down type of man with a barge pole for at least six months, and I'm keeping that promise. Besides, I'm fake dating his brother. That's a big whole mess if ever there was one.

I walk into the room and the shower is running. *Oh God*, I hope Dan wasn't serious about me joining him in the shower. I don't want it. Luckily, any fears I have are assuaged by a giggly woman who comes running out of the shower room naked.

"Kelli!" *Ugh. You have to be kidding me.* The two of them haven't lasted five minutes. "What are you doing?" To think I was just contemplating what a good, well-behaved, sensible woman I've been, and how proud Kelli would be, when all the time *she* was fucking Dan in my shower. *Unbelievable.*

"Shit, sorry, Pen. I was already in the shower, and he joined me. It wasn't planned or anything."

*Sure, whatever.*

She stands there dripping wet, her hands covering her ample assets.

"That's okay," I reply with a sigh. I grab my robe off the bed and hand it to her. "Just don't let his family catch you. I've no idea how I could explain *that*."

Dan strolls out, butt naked. Wow. I'd completely forgotten about one of the main reasons that people always come back for more. He is *packing*. "Hey, Pen, thanks for the beach. You did so good. Mom's convinced I picked a nice girl this time." Kelli throws him a dirty look. What an asshole thing to say. "Oh, come on, K. You don't think I'm seeing you because you're a nice girl, do you? Not after what we just did in the shower." *Eww*. I'm going to have to disinfect the bathroom twice over the minute those two are gone.

People always find it adorable that Dan calls them by one letter initials, but in reality, it's because he can't remember their names. He's got a whole bunch of partners he refers to as 'babe' or 'sweetie'. I can't even imagine what that does to your self-esteem.

*Oh, Kelli, honey, what have you done?*

She giggles again, grabs her bikini, which is hanging off an expensive-looking, fake Greek sculpture, and disappears back in to get dressed.

He grabs the towel from my hand and dries his crotch with it. "Could you not −?" I snap.

He looks up and sees me staring in distaste at his groin "Jealous, Pen?" He chuckles, handing me back the towel and waving his dick around like a little helicopter. "Sorry… You were saying?"

"Could you not fuck my best friend in my shower, please? It's…unsavory."

"Unsavory? Who says 'unsavory'? You are something else, Pretty Penny. I like that. Unsavory. Well, sorry," he adds, in the worst English accent. "One shall endeavor to fuck one's best friend's best friend elsewhere in the future."

I love it when he calls me his best friend. It makes me feel all fuzzy and loved. Doesn't get him off the hook, but my anger dissipates somewhat.

He continues to dry himself in front of me, either completely oblivious to my discomfort at the sight of his naked body or he simply doesn't care. It's almost like he enjoys it…watching me squirm.

"Are you good?" I ask. It comes out before I even think about if it's the right moment or whatever. It's been weighing on me ever since I heard his parents talking, loudly, about some article online. *"Debauchery,"* his mother said, as she read the story out loud to his father. *"Thank Christ he found that nice girl and is finally settling down so we don't ever have to read any of this trash again."*

He pauses. "I'm not *bad*. I'm in therapy."

"You would tell me, though, right?"

His eyes mist up. "Sure," he says, his voice cracking as he says it. He coughs. "Promise."

I pull him into my arms. "I'm here if you need me."

He hugs me, and I forget for an instant that he doesn't have a stitch of clothing on.

"Hey, Penny," says Pace's voice from behind me. *Crap.* "Oh sorry, wow, sorry."

I turn to look but he's already gone. "I should...uh, see what he wants. It might be important, or something," I say to Dan, releasing the hug and running out onto the balcony. "Pace?"

He has a face like thunder on him. "I'm so sorry. I didn't mean to... I should have knocked. I didn't think that you were—"

That man is so cute when he's angry—all huffy and stompy and not at all menacing.

"No problem. You weren't interrupting anything. What can I do for you?"

"Oh, I *was* interrupting." He frowns. "I wanted to apologize for what I said at the beach, about the puppy. It isn't your responsibility. I'll take care of him." I don't see why he needed to tell me that straight away or apologize. He didn't say anything that wasn't true. "And what I said about your breasts... I'm sorry for mentioning them or looking at them or whatever I might have done that could have offended you." He blushes wildly again and looks at his feet, trying to hide it.

He's so endearing. I'm suddenly filled with the urge to hug him, too. Is it weird to press my body against his after my clinch with his naked brother?

I resist the desire to comfort him with a full body embrace and go for the hand rub on the arm instead. The ambience right now is awkward enough.

It's sweet that he popped by, though. He's finding excuses to talk to me, and it tickles me. Am I reading too much into this? What if I'm seeing things that aren't there? The conflict of emotions toys with my brain. Normally I just say stuff, get it off my chest, but I'm playing this game of cat and mouse, and I can't decide which of us is which.

Plus, this whole situation is complicated enough without me adding an actual love interest of my own to the mix. Good God, Kelli was right. I can't be trusted. I fall for the first guy who comes along. I'll be on one knee proposing within a day.

"Thank you. How about we share the job, one big, happy family."

He throws me a wry smile. "Family?"

"The whole future sister-in-law thing. Got to keep it authentic." His face drops and so does my gut.

I was right. He *does* like me.

*Stay strong, Penny. You've got this. You can resist this man, and any others who come your way.* Single and independent. That's the way it has to be.

Why does it feel so bad, though, if it's what I'm supposed to be doing? Damn it, I need Kelli by my side and not under my fiancé. She'd keep me on the straight and narrow.

I need help, before I crack and do something stupidly delicious with this irresistibly gorgeous man.

# Chapter Six

*Pace*

The whole table is silent when Penny talks. Whether it's just because we're all nosy, wanting to find out who this woman is and how she has captured my brother's heart or because she's so captivating when she speaks, I don't know. The whole engagement thing is a lie, but the way he looks at her, the way he is around her, like she's the fucking queen, I've never seen that.

My brother's an actor, but he's not *that* good an actor.

"Our…" — she pauses, as if she's searching for the right word — "foster dad was a DJ. Well, he still is. The kind that you book for weddings and birthdays. I'd take his gear and go out into the garage and record my mixes onto my MP3 player then I'd mix them again on my computer. He has thousands of vinyls, going back years — things you can't find online."

"You're a foster kid? I've never met a foster kid before," says Emma, leaning in on her elbows, opening her mouth to ask a million more questions. *Fuck*. My sister has always been too fucking direct and embarrassingly curious for her own good.

"Emma, seriously? I'm so sorry," I butt in before anybody else gets any ideas about pursuing this line of conversation. My mother has already been giving some serious side-eye at my dad, who—in his defense—is totally oblivious to it.

Her darling Dan married to a foster child? Not on her watch.

Penny turns to me, winks and smiles. "No problem. I get it. My foster family took me in when I was seven. Kelli joined us a couple of years later, and we shared a room right up until we left at sixteen." Kelli grins and scrunches up her nose. The two of them are more like siblings than Dan and I. "Dave is more of a father than my own. That's why I hesitated about calling him my dad. My birth parents never gave me up for adoption officially, but he and Trish are the closest thing I have to a mum and a dad. Where was I now?"

"You were telling us how you became a DJ."

"Yes, right, sorry. I went pro at sixteen. I, uh, well...I'm 'DJ NYB' to the outside world, but I also work under another name."

"LazrBoy," says Dan, looking up from his phone for a second, finally listening to the conversation.

My sister's head swivels around so fast that she almost cricks her neck. "What?"

"LazrBoy," repeats Dan, as if it's the most normal thing in the world for his fake fiancée to be one of the most successful male DJs of the last ten years.

"LazrBoy. Like, *the* LazrBoy," asks Emma, her eyes popping out of her head.

*Holy shit. Penny's talented. And she's loaded, too.* Like, I thought my family was pretty rich, and there's my brother who's a step or two up from us on the tax ladder, but she has to be several notches above him.

She nods, giving the same weary smile she probably gives everybody who discovers this about her. "Yup."

My mother, who has been quietly listening in to the conversation without interruption, suddenly decides to join in. "And is this Laser-person any good?"

"Mom!" says Emma. "LazrBoy is like *the* DJ. He has a TikTok challenge that's been going on for two years. He's played Coachella and Glastonbury and —"

My mom's interest is piqued. "Well, that's nice," she says, her eyes glowing with dollar signs. She goes back to nonchalantly eating her dinner and occasionally feeding pasta and chicken to the puppy at her feet, but I saw the glimmer of a smile on her face.

All bets are off as to whether Mom likes Penny. It's official. We can book the church. The wedding is most definitely on.

The conversation dies down, and we all tuck into the food in front of us, but I can't help side-eyeing my brother.

How does he know Penny? He doesn't date rich, successful people. It's not his thing. He likes to be the one in control.

But she's sleeping with him, and I'm pretty sure he's fucking her friend, too.

She just doesn't come across as the type of woman who would be into what he's into. Anybody who gets involved with my brother finds out pretty quickly, if not instantaneously, that they're not exclusive — and they never will be.

I shift in my seat. Why do I care? There's no logical reason why I should even consider protecting this woman from my brother. She signed the damned contract. You get what you pay for, and when it comes to my brother, that normally involves a certain amount of sleaze. I love him. He's my twin. But that man can be a menace when it comes to the people he's involved with. Family included.

Penny catches my glance and I realize that I'm staring at her again, lost in my chain of thought. She winks at me for the second time today and something stirs in my loins. *Fuck.* I'm kidding myself if I don't know exactly why this woman gives me all the feels.

I need to chill. I am not going to pick up the pieces, especially when family is involved. She can dig herself out of the shithole she has leaped into feet first.

I watch the two of them playing their little game.

Dan grabs Penny's hand as she's reaching for the wine, kisses it then grabs the bottle, serving her a glass. And, exactly as predicted, she falls for his charms.

Emma turns to me, rolls her eyes and pretends to be sick. She has worked it out, too. I can be thankful for one ally, at least. Mom and Dad are entirely oblivious to Dan's faults, and his team is paid to be on his side.

This holiday is going to be one long painful, stupid Danfest. I should have known. When has my life been anything else?

* * * *

*Penny*

"Do you ever feel like you're too young for all this? It seems like only a couple of years ago we were at school being kids and now we're supposed to be grown-ups. All my friends are spending their summers getting drunk in Ibiza, but I'm here, pretending to marry your brother. It's a lot."

Pace raises an eyebrow and picks up a card. "Nobody's forcing you to stay. You can go when you want."

I stick out my bottom lip. "You don't want me to stay."

"I want you to show me your hand so I can beat your ass at poker."

I put my cards face down on the table and take another sip of my drink. "We should have made this more interesting."

"Strip poker?"

*Wow.* The last time I played strip poker, it did not end well. And by that I mean it ended spectacularly, orgasmically naked and in bed with someone who ended up breaking my heart, as men like to do. I shuffle in my seat. This is not the straight and narrow. This is fore-foreplay. I shouldn't have gotten so hot and bothered over the sparkle in his eye when he said it, but damn, I'm tempted to say yes.

It's been less than one day and I am already smitten. I don't have a chance of resisting for two weeks. I cross my legs and think sensible thoughts like 'finding the real me' and 'loving myself before I love others'. *God*, I'm a walking motivational poster.

"I meant we should have bet actual money instead of gummy bears, but when you're sitting naked in front of me, you're going to regret ever suggesting that idea."

He puts a hand to his chest, throws his head back and laughs, mocking me. "You think you can beat *me*?"

"Maybe?" I smile, biting at my lip. This silly flirting has been going on ever since he sat down in front of me with a pack of cards and suggested I do something more interesting than just stare out at the dark crashing waves. "Scared?"

"Of losing against you and showing you my naked butt? No. You've seen the carbon copy already, so you know what you're in for. I'm more concerned about you stripping down to your underwear only a few feet away from my parents' bedroom and having to explain that to my mom."

"We could blame it on the tequila." I raise my glass and take another sip of the very strong cocktail that Pace concocted from what he found in the bar.

"It would be my fault. It's always my fault."

"You think you're that important?" I say. He raises an eyebrow. "My mum — my foster mum — used to say it when one of us claimed that she was singling them out. *'You think you're so important that I'm going to spend all of my time on just you. I have other kids to tell off. I nag you all equally.'*"

He chuckles and scratches his stubble. He was perfectly well-shaven this morning, but I like this look on him. It's a touch more rebellious than the clean-cut image he had at the airport when we met. Then he lets out a sad little sigh.

"She sounds like a great mom."

"She is. I couldn't have picked a better one."

I know about his mum. I know what her narcissism did to Dan, and I can only imagine what it has done to Pace. I want so much to comfort him, to tell him that it's okay to hate her, but I'm sworn to secrecy on the matter. It's not my place to talk about his family. That's reserved for Dan and me.

He picks up a card. I've no idea if I have a good hand or not. It's been an eternity since I've played cards.

Reece was obsessed with his computer games, and my job doesn't leave a lot of time for sitting around at night with friends — not since I've been on the road, anyway.

The last year has been gigging and more gigging. I haven't had time to sit and create for a while. When I wasn't at work, I was being the doting girlfriend. Before I moved down from Manchester to live with Reece, I was constantly traveling to and from his house every opportunity I got. I spent more time in trains, private cars and airports than I care to think about.

All I wanted to do was make music. That's how I started, and that's how I made my first million. Then I decided to try to be me — a girl DJ. Shock, horror! Can you imagine such a thing? No longer hidden behind a mask. '*Real*' me hasn't done so well. The lack of support dried up my creative juices a while back, so now it's just gig after gig of playing LazrBoy with a stupid mask on my head and releasing a crowd-pleasing over-produced hit every few months. Anonymity guaranteed.

I need to get back to making music that moves people. It's not as if I can't afford to take some time for me. I just seem to have gotten lost on the way. Being a grown-up sucks. I'd give it all up if I could move back into my parents' loft bedroom and mix all day.

Pace clicks his fingers softly under my nose. "Penny. Wake up. It's your turn. Let's see your hand, then." He winks at me, an expectant smile on his face. Boy, is he going to be disappointed.

"Sorry." I have a pair of sixes. *Thank God we didn't go the strip poker route.* I place them down on the table.

His face is a picture. I really had him going. "No way. I totally thought you were going to whip my ass."

"Nope. I learned to bluff when I was twelve. That's the only thing I'm good at when it comes to playing poker."

"And to think you wanted to strip." He gives a little chuckle and leans back into his chair, his eyes going up and down my body. Yeah, he's thinking about what's under my pajamas.

"I did not. That was your idea. I wanted to lose all my money to you."

He grins. "That would help pay for college."

Here's me complaining about being all rich and successful and this guy is just trying to get through his studies without ending up in debt.

"Yeah. So, medical school. That's hard work, huh?"

He shrugs. "I don't get a lot of sleep, but it's been my dream my whole life. I couldn't give it up, not after all these years of wanting it."

"So you still live with your parents?"

He lets out the deepest, most miserable sigh. "It's the only thing I'm good at or passionate about. Unfortunately, it doesn't exactly pay the bills yet, at least not enough to get my own place."

"And your parents don't want to help set you up somewhere?" I don't add, *'because they can certainly afford to'*, but he must know I'm thinking it.

"I've..." He pushes his glasses up his nose and chooses his words. "I've always been a bit of a disappointment to them. There's Dan with all his money and fame and success, then there's me and my ten years of college. Even my sister has more success on Instagram than I do in life. My parents are like, *'we'll be proud of you when you've got that diploma in your hand'*. And now he's turned up with a beautiful fiancée, and that makes me look even more like a loser."

"I'm sure you could get any woman you want."
How is this man still single? Okay, yeah, admittedly
he's a little tongue-tied and talks way too much about
*Star Wars* for a lot of people's liking, but he's going to
be a doctor one day, a pretty attractive one, too. That
has to be a selling point.

His eyes widen at just the idea of such a thing. "Me?
No. They only want me for one thing…my brother's
phone number."

There he goes again, putting himself down. "Yeah,
because women hate handsome medical students who
can make delicious cocktails."

"You think I'm handsome?"

I purse my lips. "Don't push your luck, Pacey Scott.
I already let you beat me at cards. And, for what it's
worth, you should take a step back occasionally and
take a good look at yourself. You might find that the
person you see isn't as worthless as you — or anybody
else, for that matter — make him out to be."

He leans forward, picks up his cocktail and looks out
at the waves, crashing against the sand in the
moonlight, silent tears forming in his eyes.

He's not just handsome. He's sublime. Perfect in
every way. If I weren't banned from even looking twice
at men at the moment, I'd make a move in a second.

But I'm not, so he's just good company. That's all it
is. No kissing and no peeking to see what's under those
tan Bermuda shorts. I've seen the mirror image version,
though, and it did not disappoint. It's got me
wondering if *everything* is identical when it comes to
twins.

*"Messy and complicated."* That what Kelli had told me
earlier. *"Don't go there,"* she'd added, pointing her
perfectly manicured finger at me and waving it around

for good measure. "*I'm warning you, Penny. I'm going to kick your arse if you even look in the direction of that man. He's problematic, and you know it.*" This is coming from the woman who had sex with my fake fiancé only hours after meeting him, despite my advice to the contrary. I'm starting to seriously question her judgment, especially as she and Dan disappeared straight after dinner and haven't been seen since.

Unfortunately, despite her behavior, she has a valid point, so I say nothing. I stop flirting, sip my drink and watch the waves until Pace gathers himself, shuffles and deals the cards again. If I can't kiss those beautiful lips, trace the stubble on his chin and check out his naked butt under the Spanish moonlight, I can at least enjoy being beaten by him at cards.

Like I said, he's good company. And that'll do me for now.

# Chapter Seven

*Day Two*
*Penny*

Rich people, when it comes down to it, are exactly the same as everybody else, but they just wear more expensive clothes. Take, for example, this ridiculous 'sports day' that we appear to have been signed up for. Karl had announced it last night. A group from each house along millionaire's row is competing to win a trophy which — to all appearances — is a cheap plastic piece of crap from the local supermarket.

You wouldn't have thought it interested them to be forced to race around, their legs tied together, or jump along the beach in potato sacks, but they are as up for it as anybody I know, if not more. What they lack in experience they make up for in fierce competitiveness.

Another thing about rich people is that they do *not* like to lose.

I like to think I'm not like them — that I'm the young girl from a working-class background who grew up in a foster home — but on paper, I'm as rich as they come. I put my money to work then I forget about it. I release a song, it becomes a hit then I hand all the details over to my accountant. It's probably not the wisest move on my part, but it's a lot easier for me to cope.

"What are you thinking about so intensely?" asks Kelli as she lies down on the lounger next to mine. She's wearing a pair of those leggings that lift and support, with the matching bra-shaped top. They have molded her to perfection. I look down at my Queen T-shirt and denim shorts. Perhaps I could have made a touch more of an effort. Hey, I shaved my legs. That has to count for something.

"I was thinking about how it's so unfair that some people have so much money and others don't."

"Well, you don't have that problem." She side-eyes me. Our difference in financial status has never affected our friendship, but then I'd never expect Kelli to pay for something she couldn't afford. We live cheaply, and when we don't, I'm the one who pays. It's never been an issue, not for me, at least. She's my sister and that's just what you do for family.

"I know. Pacey's really unhappy living with his parents. It just seems so unfair that he can't get his own place."

She gasps. "I don't believe you, woman. Don't you dare fall for that guy and buy him a house."

"Says the girl who is sleeping with Perfect Husband Dan Scott."

She giggles. "I know, right? Can you believe it?"

"That you have genitals and that Dan wants to sleep with you? What a fucking shocker."

It would be more surprising if he *hadn't* bedded her by now.

"Okay, no need to be such a bitch about it. Are you jealous or what? If I'm overstepping my boundaries, I can just walk away."

*Oh God, no thank you.* "No worries there. Dan and I aren't like that. You just have to remind yourself that Dan will never fall in love, never settle down and will cheat on you, if you can even call it that, because the man never commits to anything. And you won't leave him. Nobody who ever sleeps with that man leaves him. He reels you in then breaks your heart. That's the only way you get out."

She narrows her eyes at me. "He seems pretty committed to you."

"That's different. We have a certain…bond. Like you and me."

She leans closer, whispers, "Don't fall in love with Pacey with the sad eyes, either. It'll only end up breaking your heart, too. *Again.*"

"But then you and I can mutually console each other with cocktails. We can wallow in our misery together."

"Nah, Dan's going to fall in love with me. I can feel it." *Oh, good Lord.* She's in way deeper than I thought. Nothing I say is going to convince her that she's making a terrible mistake.

And nothing she says is going to work on me. Ridiculous romantics, the pair of us.

"It's starting. It's starting," says Emma as she throws herself down onto the lounger and points to the beach.

"What?"

"The tug of war. They've split the street into two groups then they're going to whittle them down. J.F. is competing." She grins about as wide as an eighteen-year-old girl can when she's in love. "It's the final event. Only a couple of points in it between us and J F.'s family, so this determines today's winner."

It hasn't escaped anybody's attention that Jean-François from the rather upscale Parisian family staying two doors down has caught Emma's eye. Her presence on the beach has been constant since she met him the day before, and her bikinis are getting skimpier by the hour, much to her mother's disapproval. Apparently I'm supposed to be dressing up more, and Emma is supposed to be dressing down. Terri spends way too much of her time thinking about other people's clothes.

It also hasn't escaped mine and Kelli's attention that Dan and Pace are representing our house. *Oh my God.* It's all I can do not to stare. The shirts are off in the afternoon heat, and the boys are already glowing with sweat as they get into position.

It's fucking Christmas on the beach, and Santa has *delivered.*

"So they just pull?" says Kelli, her tongue dragging on the floor at the sight of Dan's tight, muscular body as he begins to take the weight.

"You see the little ribbon in the middle? They have to pull that over the line in the sand," I reply, trying to keep myself together in front of this beautiful sight.

Pace wraps his large hands around the rope and leans back. The muscles in his arms instantly double in size. *Fuck.* He hides them well under his freshly pressed cotton shirts.

I've never seen him and Dan lined up like that. Pace is actually the larger of the two, as far as muscles go, and he looks positively apelike next to his tanned, waxed twin. Not that he's particularly hairy, just a delicate tuft on his chest and a soft duvet covering his arms and legs.

The referee blows his whistle and they start to pull.

*Jesus.* It's a glorious thing to see on a Spanish beach on a hot day.

"Drinks, ladies?" Karl walks past with a pitcher of lemonade on a tray. The three of us lean to look around him. He shuffles along to move out of our way. "What are we watching? *Holy Mother of God!*" He slumps down onto a fourth lounger as his eyes dilate at the view.

"I've never seen anything so...exquisite," adds Kelli, unable to look away. "Go on, Dan, Pacey. You've got this!" she shouts as our lads and their team pull the ribbon over the line. They jump up and down, high-five each other and add a few chest-bumps for good measure.

Karl does a loud finger whistle, and the lads look our way.

"Woohooo!" I shout, as Dan and Pacey wave at us. Jean-François gives Emma a timid wave, too. Bless him, he looks like a toothpick surrounded by all those grown men.

Emma doesn't care. She sits up and blows him a kiss. "*Aller*, Jean-François," she shouts then falls back in a fit of giggles.

The winning team is divided into two teams of four for the second round. We sip lemonade and prepare ourselves for another bout of cheerleading—if you can call it that. Lusting would be more truthful, if a little less appropriate.

Our little support group has multiplied as the French install themselves in the row of loungers. Chef joins us, leaning over Karl's lounger and kissing him on the top of the head. Even he's got shorts on today. I've yet to see him out of his uniform and out of the kitchen. I love that Dan's family includes the people who work for him, too. I'm not comfortable with the whole 'employee-employer' situation. I only have a PA, and my stylist is my best friend.

The whistle blows and this time it goes much quicker. Our lads, their feet firmly entrenched in the sand, make short shrift of their opponents, sending them to the ground with a few tugs of the rope.

Our corner of the street are all up on our feet and ready to cheer them on for the final tug.

Jean-François raises a hand. His brother is limping rather strangely. We all take five, waiting quietly as Pace checks out the French lad's ankle. Whatever it is, if they can't get someone to replace him, they're out of the game.

Dan looks up and sees everybody's disappointed faces. He points at Chef, beckons him over. I guess he *is* French, so why not. The crowd wants a final.

The crowd roars as the whistle blows. Dan and Pace, now on their own, are exhausted. They've been doing this for ten minutes now. Chef is doing the work of two men next to Jean-François but he's raring to go. Karl is even more implicated now, screaming and yelling for both teams. We all know who he wants to win, but hey, his boss is out there, too.

Despite their best efforts, though, Chef and J.F. aren't any match for the twins. They pull the rope over the line for the third and final time and the whole crowd erupts. Every single woman in the place runs over to congratulate the boys. You'd think they'd just won some major sports event from everyone's behavior.

Kelli and I have to fight our way through the crowd of tanned bikini-clad bodies to get to them. Kelli jumps into Dan's arms and Pace scoops me up and spins me around. He grabs onto me so tight, yelling in my ear, then nuzzles into my neck, his lips brushing against my skin as he takes a breath.

Karl wolf-whistles us from twenty feet away as he comforts Chef, and we all freeze, look at each other. Kelli and I instantly jump from one man to the other. *Crap*. That was a bit close. There's like a million phones pointed at us right now, all ready to fill social media with photos and videos of everybody's *amazing* holiday in Spain with Dan Scott, superstar. This is not the moment to be forgetting our roles here—or mine, at least.

I slip into my perfect portrayal of celebrity girlfriend and snuggle up to my man. The smell of Pace's aftershave tinged with sea salt and sweat has impregnated into my top and I can still feel the sting from the bristles on his chin as he rubbed his face against mine.

When will this longing end? Will there ever be a time when I'm not constantly thinking about him?

\* \* \* \*

*Pacey*

Settling down onto the lounger after a hard day's toiling on the beach, a glass of chilled lemonade in my hand from Karl, I close my eyes, allowing my muscles to relax. That was hard work—harder than my daily workout.

"I can't believe our family won. We never win anything and *never* together," I say to Penny, who grabbed the lounger next to mine when Kelli went off to celebrate with Dan away from the cameras and inquisitive eyes.

"I'm just glad everybody else did the work and I can claim all the glory. I was pretty hopeful Bob was going to come out of his shell and turn out to be an iron man," replies Penny, with a grin.

My dad is sitting three loungers down with his nose stuck in a good book. He has been of no use whatsoever to our team today.

"Yeah, no, no luck there. Dad hasn't moved since he sold his company four years ago. Made a fortune in mechanical car parts then gave it up so he and mum could retire and enjoy their lives." Some might argue that spending the last twenty or thirty years of your life with your nose in a book, ignoring the world around you, doesn't exactly qualify as 'enjoying life', but I wouldn't mind it.

I've had way more fun with a book than I've ever had with real people. A well-chosen book rarely disappoints, but people let me down all the time.

"So did you see me in the sack race? I rocked it, as usual."

"Good in the sack, are you?" I reply without thinking. *Ugh.* Penny brings out the Dan in me. Twenty-one years of having a brother who takes every conversation down to his level and I've managed to avoid it so far. It's like he mind-melded me on the plane over here and filled my brain with the dirtiest one-liners. "Sorry. I didn't mean to—"

"Don't apologize." She smiles at me. "It was funny. And yes, I was top of my class several years running in the sack race. Well, I was nine years old, but I've still got it. I was also counting on the beautiful people not wanting to fall flat on their faces, which gave me the advantage. I didn't care if I ate sand."

"Wow, so heavy tactics were involved. Sneaky. Dan made me do the tug of war because somebody told him that men pulling ropes is hot."

From the crowd's reaction, it was very hot. And from the look on Penny's face when she leaped into my arms at the end, she definitely enjoyed it. No regrets there.

"That would be Kelli. And yes it was." She blushes, as if she's reliving it in her mind.

"That good, huh?" She nods, biting her lip. "And you don't mind Dan and your friend uh...getting together."

She frowns. "They can do what they like." How is she not pissed that the guy she's sleeping with is also sleeping with her best friend? How is this *normal* to her?

"Whatever. It's weird."

"Pace." She lowers her voice. "You get that it's fake, right? That we're not actually together. *Jesus*, Pace, you don't think I'm actually fucking Dan, do you?" She shakes her head, then laughs so loudly that everybody turns to look.

"Uh, yeah." I look down at my body. Okay, so I'm not exactly as skinny as Dan, but we've still got the same body, and the same face. "What's wrong with my brother?"

"I love your brother with all my heart, as I'm sure you do, but let's be honest. He makes Leonardo DiCaprio look virginal." Everybody is still looking at us, so I throw my hand over my mouth to stop myself from laughing. *Holy fuck.* She's not wrong, but still, that's harsh. "Not, you know, that that's a problem. Don't let it be said that you can't freely express your love the way you see fit. I just don't want him freely expressing it anywhere near *my* lady-parts."

This does it for me and I crack up, sending Penny into a fit of giggling, too. "What are you two up to?" says Dan, looking like he's fresh out of the shower. He slides in between us and ousts me off the lounger.

"I was just telling Pace here how good I am in the sack," says Penny with a sly grin. Dan raises an eyebrow. "The potato sack, of course."

"Well, keep it down. Mom's watching."

I step back from the lounger and Dan rolls onto Penny, hovers over her and asks, "I can kiss you, right? It's cool? I brushed my teeth and everything. No tongue, I swear."

This elicits even more giggles from her. "Sure, whatever."

I turn away. I don't need to see it, nor do I want to. I don't get how Penny can't be totally not into my brother and yet she lets him kiss her like that.

My rage gets the better of me and I sneak a peek at the two of them. He barely brushes her lips. You couldn't tell if you weren't right where I'm standing, but he's hardly even kissing her at all—just enough for any stragglers on our part of the beach to snap an elicit photo.

The rage that was building in my gut subsides. Whatever is happening between these two, it's not happening right now. Hope springs eternal, and that's all I've got right now, a little trust and a little hope.

# Chapter Eight

*Penny*

Showered, primped and preened, our glamorous neighbors come back out onto the beach looking to continue the party. Staff bring out food from every home, trays and trays of gluten-free, vegan avocado toast. Unfortunately, the local DJ hired to be in charge of music for the day has started to wind up and doesn't look like he's intending to stick around.

"*Oh my God*, Penny, you should totally do a session," says Kelli. She turns to Dan, tapping him on the arm until he puts down his phone and listens to her. "She should do a session. Get the DJ to let her use his stuff. Pen, go get your computer."

*My best friend and my biggest fan.*

I don't have much. My computer and my headphones are the only real gear I brought, but most of my mixes are on there, so we're good to go. This guy has used his computer all day, so it's simply going to be a case of switching from one to the other. It's not exactly Ibiza, but these guys aren't expecting DJ royalty — even though that's what they're getting.

I might not be spectacular when it comes to relationships, but when it comes to my job, I'm simply one of the best.

"Oh I don't know. You know how people get with their gear. I don't want to step on anybody's toes."

Dan calls Karl over, pulls his wallet out of his pocket and hands it to him. "Pay what it takes to hire that guy's equipment for the night." Karl shrugs. From the wad of cash that Dan has in his wallet, if that DJ has a lick of sense, he can replace his entire kit with the fee Karl's willing to offer him.

Kelli smiles and Dan throws her a wink. Maybe he's changed after all. Maybe he sees the beauty and love that I see in her.

I stand up and wipe the sand from my legs. "I guess I'll get my computer, then."

Kelli claps her hands together. "Yes!"

I set myself up and prepare some songs. I start with one of my favorites — literally one of my own songs. Well, LazrBoy's, in any case. It's a club mix I use when I'm being him. People are already up and dancing. I love that my music gets people on their feet. As I get into my set, I remember why I adore this job. Getting the crowd to sing along, to cheer for the songs they've been waiting to hear. It's an amazing feeling. I throw in some classics, with a little LazrBoy twist. Hopefully nobody out here has a good ear. Anybody who has been to one of my sets as him would recognize some of these in an instant.

"You want a drink?" asks Pace, placing his hand on my back to get my attention. I lift my headphones from one ear and smile.

"Sure."

"Sorry my brother made you work."

"Are you kidding? This is what I do. I was starting to miss it already." This is where I belong. Pace has been sitting with Gus on his lap for the last hour, if you don't count the time Kelli dragged him onto the beach for a dance. "I'm still up for a game of cards, though, after this, if you want." His smile widens. I get the feeling Mr. Pacey Scott doesn't like sharing me with everybody else.

I do a good hour and a half, including a little something I threw together this morning with a sample that I made of Emma when she wanted to know how I work my magic. Her face lights up when she realizes that *she* is the star of the song. Jean-François doesn't know what he's got himself into. That girl is a firecracker, and tonight she is lit.

I bring it down a notch for the last couple of songs. Dan sneaks up behind me and dances with me for the last one, twirling me around and snuggling up to me. He's warm and comforting...my big teddy bear. "Thanks for doing this, Pen. You killed it. I'm going to another party with Kelli and some of the others. Do you want to come?"

"Nah, I'm exhausted, thanks. I'll pack all this up and head on in. Thanks, Dan, I needed this."

"I feel like we both did," he replies with a satisfied smile.

"It was awesome." I peck him on the cheek. "I'm so glad we did this — the trip. I missed you."

"Missed you, too. It was fate." I nod and he twirls me around one last time, pecks me on the nose and heads off. He seems okay — as okay as Dan ever is, which is still on a completely different level to everybody else's average state.

I find Pace on the balcony, drinks ready, cards out. He is *eager*.

"You didn't want to go to the party with Dan and everybody?"

He looks affronted. "We had a date, didn't we? I mean, if you want to go…"

"Oh no, I love our little rendezvous. Don't know if I'm going to be good company, though, I'm exhausted." His face gets even sadder. '*Don't fall for those puppy dog eyes,*' that's what Kelli said, but it's hard to resist.

"I saw you dancing with Dan," he says. Ah, so that's what the moping is all about. I can tell him a million times but he's never going to stop being jealous of his brother. The two of them are more like rivals than brothers — little digs and snipes all the time. If only they could see the good in each other as I do.

"Get up." He furrows his brow. "Come on, and get up."

I pull him into my bedroom and open up my computer, choosing one of the soulful little numbers I finished up my set with. I wrap my hands around his neck, pulling him close. His body is warm and welcoming. He wraps his arms instinctively around my waist, his fingers gripping gently onto my lower back. Always the gentleman.

Our eyes lock. He swallows. He is awkward and smitten and eager to kiss me. At least that's how *I* feel right now, and if his eyes are telling me anything, it's that he feels the exact same way.

"Emma, is that you playing music?" His mum's voice breaks our bubble. "Pacey. It's late. You're disturbing your father's sleep." The sound of footsteps coming down the balcony throws us into a panic. Pacey dives behind my bed and I dive onto it.

She pops her head in the window as if that's completely normal—not a knock or a thought that I might not be decent. Her night cream is smudged all over her face, which doesn't disguise her pissed-off frown.

"Penny? Is that you making all that noise?"

"Mrs. Scott, Terri, I'm so sorry. I was putting my computer away and I accidentally put the music on. My apologies to Bob."

"Oh, no problem dear. Where's Dan?"

"He's helping clear up after the party. I'm sure he'll be here soon."

"Good, good. Well, I'm back off to bed. Goodnight, Penny."

She wanders back to bed, and I lean over and look down at Pacey cowering on the floor. "I'm sure she wouldn't have minded you being here."

"She would have minded me dancing with you."

*Or kissing me?* "Where were we?"

"I was about to whip your pretty ass at poker."

"Ah, so it's like that, is it? Maybe I've been bluffing. Maybe tonight I'll whip *your* ass."

He chuckles and tips his head to one side. "Bless you. You're so cute when you're about to lose your shirt."

I head on out of the room, then turn to point as he gets up from his hiding place. "That's it. I'm definitely going to beat you now."

He shakes his head and makes a dismissive gesture with his hand. The moment is gone. We're back to pretending to be friends. Something has changed, though. An idea has been explored…a moment shared.

I'm not going to kiss Pacey Scott tonight, but I *am* going to kiss him. It's just a matter of time. I know it, and he knows it. He's just going to have to get over the fact that for the next six days I'm going to be kissing his brother, too.

*Awkward.*

# Chapter Nine

*Day Three*
*Penny*

Some things I know to be true, and when it comes to body confidence, it's literally just that. Confidence. I don't often have it. In fact, I hide my body away more than anything else, but you can't do that in a bikini — especially this bikini. So my plan is to get my shit together. I need to look like I *know* I'm the prettiest girl here and hope that that's the vibe they're going to get. I'm dating one of the hottest guys on the planet. That has to count for something, right?

Kelli and Emma got the memo. We stroll out of the changing rooms ready to kill, like some kind of elite group of spies who can take on the world — hands on hips, heads held high.

It didn't start that way. A day out with Dan involves having to get up at some ungodly hour. Okay, it was eight a.m. but it felt very, very early after a second night of tequila and poker with my *close friend* Pacey.

Before leaving, we all had to go get a makeover from Dan's stylist, including the devastating discovery that if I wanted to wear the bikini that Dan had picked out of my suitcase for me today — one of Kelli's favorites — I had to shave parts of me that should never see daylight. To sum it up, I'm me, but not really. Me in a pretty, shaved, made-up shell.

Admittedly, we all look fantastic. I have no idea how I'm going to *stay* fantastic in a waterpark. Let's face it. In about ten minutes, my look is going to go from devastatingly gorgeous to drowned rat, but for now, I'm owning it.

The gentlemen are waiting for us. Dan and his entourage, plus a bodyguard that Karl has hired for the day. Never has a six-foot monster-sized man looked so disappointed to have to follow a bunch of twenty-somethings around a water park for a day. Jean-François is also there, having now become a permanent fixture in the household. He looks like he's going to cry from the joy of being with us. A beautiful girl invites him out for the day with her very famous movie-star brother. His mentions are going to *explode*.

"Wow," says Dan.

"Thank... Oh." *Crap.* He's staring at Kelli, his tongue hanging out, his short shorts bursting at the seams. *Cool, okay. Awkward.*

"For what it's worth, I think you're stunning," quips Pace, winking at me.

"Fuck, sorry, Pen. You look amazing. You always look amazing." Dan cringes at his faux pas.

"Too little, too late," I reply, laughing. In their quest to see who can look us over without being caught looking us over, neither of the Scott brothers has noticed that their sister has looped her arm through her new boyfriend's and slipped away while she had the chance. "Is that boy of Emma's trustworthy?" I ask. I don't like to tell on her, but I don't think either of them wants to have to tell their mother that they've lost her.

"*Jesus.* Karl, go find her, follow her and don't get too close, just enough to let me know what she's up to." Dan's ever-suffering PA rolls his eyes and does as he is told. I've no idea how much that man is getting paid, but it clearly isn't enough.

"Looks like I'm doing the lovers' photo shoot, then," says Kelli, looking a touch displeased at having to photograph her lover with me in his arms.

The water park is huge and extremely busy. The guests are mainly European and reasonably polite when it comes to approaching Dan. That said, we definitely need the bodyguard to keep people at bay. It's not that they're menacing in any way. I don't feel threatened when I'm out and about with him. It's just that they're constantly stopping us from doing anything or going anywhere. Selfies are the thing, and if people can get one with you then they'll quite happily stand in your way and just film or photograph you.

I signed up for this. It's part of my contract, so I really need to smile more and look like I'm having just the best time. This has to bring work my way, which is a good thing, but, *oh my God*, it's so fucking tedious.

We find a quiet spot, one of many small pools where people can just hang out, and we take the opportunity to get some photos in. Kelli seems pretty keen to get this done then go off somewhere with Dan to canoodle in private. The two of them are so into each other that it's positively sickening. I mean, I'm happy for them but seriously, *chill*.

"Look to your left a little more. That's great. Now, Dan, put your hand on her thigh. A little higher. Awesome."

"We're drawing a crowd," I mutter as Dan slides his hand up my leg. I look over at Pace. He looks like he'd rather poke his eyes out with sticks than spend another minute witnessing this public display of entirely fake love.

"Almost done. Do you mind if Kelli and I — ?"

"Oh God, no. The minute I can get away from you and your crowd of adoring fans, I'll be off." He adjusts his crotch underneath me and sinks his hand lovingly under my chin. "Remember when we had that bath together and you did not stop farting?"

He chuckles. "It wasn't my fault. It was the pizza — you know how I am with gluten — and that bath was as big as this pool."

"You kept calling it my own personal Jacuzzi. I swear I've never shared a bath with anyone ever again after that. You put me right off." This makes him laugh even more and he decides to take revenge by tickling me, causing us both to sink under the water. We come back up, only this time I'm facing him. "You stink of cigarettes. Have you never heard of nicotine patches?"

He kisses me on the nose. "Women love it, and it's part of my edgy, tough-guy image. Nicotine patches don't scream guy-you-could-never-take-home-to-your-mom."

"You must be *so* good in bed to get any of them coming back for more."

He winks at me. "You should try it some time. You might be surprised."

"With you? Eww." I turn to Kelli, who has jealous steam pouring from every orifice. "Are we done yet?"

"Yes. Thanks. I think we're good," she snaps.

"Wait," says Dan, pulling me in for one last tight hug and letting rip the loudest fart. "Okay, we're good." He extricates himself from beneath me, jumps up and holds out a hand to help me out of the water.

"You're a disgusting excuse for a man."

That earns me a satisfied smile. "But you still love me."

"I don't. Okay, I do. Don't tell anybody, though. I have a reputation, you know." I step out of the water and into a towel that Pace is holding out for me. "I'll see you guys for lunch?"

We arrange to meet up at the onsite restaurant in a couple of hours and they rush off, bodyguard in tow. The things that poor man is going to have to witness today, I cannot even imagine.

"Looks like it's just you and me," says Pace, not looking entirely displeased with the way things have worked out.

"It does."

"Have you ever slept with my brother?" he says, literally out of nowhere.

*Okay.* "No, never have, never will. I told you this already, although you really don't want to believe me for some reason," I reply, mustering a smile.

He narrows his eyes. "But you said you loved him."

"The two aren't mutually exclusive. Don't *you* love him?"

"He's my twin brother. It's an unwritten law. I have to. You're under no such obligation."

"For all his faults, your brother is a good man. But, look... I don't want to talk about him all day, if that's okay. It looks like we've got the rest of the morning to discover what this place has to offer. What's your jam? Death slides? Big waves? Floating around on inflatables and sipping cocktails?"

He grins maliciously and points at the very scary slides. "I love a good scare."

I don't, I really don't, but this is supposed to be a time of trying new things and enjoying being just me, not thinking about the whole seriousness of life.

New Penny takes risks and lives life dangerously.

"Okay, but on two conditions. First, you go before me so that you're waiting at the bottom and second, if we can do them together, you hold my hand."

He tilts his head. "Are you scared?"

"I can't swim. Do I need to swim? I... Nobody ever taught me to swim."

He grabs my hand. "I'll be right there with you. It'll be fun. You'll see."

\* \* \* \*

*Pace*

I swear somebody up there is toying with me. First, they make me come to this godforsaken island with my family, then I meet the funniest, cleverest, sexiest woman in the universe who is quite possibly in love with my brother, legally obliged to date him and possibly sleeping with him, despite what she says. Then, to top it all off, we have to spend a day half-naked, splashing around in water, with her insisting that I hold her hand.

I can't get my head around what terrible thing I did to deserve this.

Did I mention that she looks sensational in a bikini? Well, she does. She looks amazing in anything, which in her case is mostly T-shirts with rock band logos emblazoned on them.

She's hot and she's doing things to me that make me want to kiss her…and I can't.

*Fuck my life*.

We climb up the first water chute and I go first, then she follows a couple of minutes after. She shoots out of the bottom of the water slide and plummets under the water. What's a decent amount of time to wait for her to pop her head out? Two seconds? Three? I step forward, just in case, and she stands up, pushes her hair out of her face, looks down and yelps.

*Oh fuck*.

Literally every knot on her bikini has come undone. It's still covering everything, well as much as that tiny piece of material covered anything in the first place. What was Dan thinking when he chose this for her? This is not a *Penny* bikini, it's a *Kelli* bikini.

I sweep her up into my arms and pull her away from the people about to land on her head then the two of us tie her back into her swimwear.

"Thank you. Oh my God, that was close."

"It's not like anybody saw." She scrunches up her brows. *Crap. I didn't mean it like that.* "Not that they weren't looking at you. Not that everybody *was* looking at you. You're beautiful. They didn't see."

She giggles. "As a doctor, do you have to announce bad news to people? Like if a family member has passed or something, do you have to tell them? Because you really need to work on using your words."

Why does my mouth not connect with my brain when I'm around this woman? I could be speaking Klingon for all the sense I make.

"You fluster me."

She giggles and pulls herself up onto the side of the pool, facing me.

"I do? I don't think I've ever flustered anybody ever. Thank you, I think." She splashes her feet in the water inches away from me, twirling her toes around the tips of my chest hair. I can't breathe. I clench my fists as I resist the temptation to touch her, to snuggle up to her, to feel her body next to mine. "Are you going to go again?"

"Huh?"

She grins at me and clicks her fingers. "Hey, Pace, come back down to earth. The slide. Are you going to go down the slide again?"

I nod and head on back up the steps, leaving her to sit and splash on the side of the pool.

The second descent is more controlled than the first. I know it now. As I shoot out of the slide and into the water, it's a much more graceful landing. Plus, I know she's watching me, so it has to look good. I make very sure to stand up straight and flick the water from my hair like a shampoo ad.

*Jesus.* What have I become that my life involves trying to impress this woman who is clearly way more into my brother than she is into me?

"Are you Dan Scott?" asks someone in a very polite New York accent. I turn to look at the woman standing a few feet away from me, and just for a moment I'm tempted to say yes. Nobody ever sees the resemblance, not straight away. Maybe she knows that he's here and she think he's me. Or maybe, without my glasses and with wet hair I look a lot more like him than I normally do.

Is this what it's like to be him? I can't lie. It feels good to be looked at the way this woman is looking at me. My conscience takes over, though. I might have the same face as the world's number one ladies' man, but I'm not him. I don't ever want to be him.

"No. Sorry."

She giggles and the sound of someone whooshing down behind us makes us both jump. I grab her and steer her to safety, which sends her into a further fit of giggles. "Are you sure? You really look like him."

I'm larger than my brother — pretty sure he only sees a gym when he has to prepare for a movie — and a lot hairier. Dan had his body hair removed by laser years ago. He wouldn't be seen dead with the rug I've got on my chest.

I glance over at Penny. She's got a face like thunder. *Whoa.* Is she jealous? "He's my brother."

"Really?" The girl turns toward her friends and gives them a thumbs-up. "Can we get a selfie?"

"Sure."

"And your number." I'm tempted, just because nobody ever asks. I don't really want her number. As soon as she finds out what I'm really like, she won't be interested anymore.

Plus, I have someone else on my mind, if not in my arms.

The girl drags me over to the edge of the pool and we climb out. I pose for a couple of selfies and we leave it at that. Unfortunately, that draws all kinds of attention to me. Other people are eyeing me up, trying to work out who I am.

"We need to get out of here," I say to Penny as she stomps over and stands sulkily by my side. She hands me a towel.

"Uh-huh. Or you could stay here and get some more photos with your adoring fans." She throws me a sour smile. *Fuck*, is she jealous? Did I do that? Did I make her jealous? I stick my hand over my mouth to hide my uncontrollable grin.

"Are you okay?"

"I'm fine." Rule seventy-two of understanding women is that when they say they're fine, they're *never* fine. "I thought you didn't like all of that, the fans and the fame."

She shivers and I wrap the towel around her shoulders and rub her back. "I don't. I was just being polite. You don't have anything against people being polite, do you?"

"No. You can do what you like." The way she says it sounds just like 'I'm fine' but with different words.

She's still shivering, so I pull her in closer. The two of us are almost naked, huddling together, skin to skin. She looks up at me, and for the second time since I met her, the urge to kiss those trembling, damp, pouty lips of hers overwhelms me — except this time my mother is nowhere to be seen.

She parts them, her face inches from mine, her gaze boring into mine. Then she lets out a defeated sigh. "We're in public. I have a contract with Dan. I can't. I signed a contract."

She pulls away, just a few inches, enough to leave room for Jesus. What would happen if I just kissed her? I'm not going to, she clearly doesn't want me to, but what would it feel like? I lick my lips and breathe, allowing my body to calm its shit. The things she does to me are not things I want to be happening when I'm only wearing bathing shorts, and I'm standing so close that she *has* to feel me stirring.

We step apart and she busies herself folding the towel and looking away from me. "We should find the others."

"Yeah."

She glances back up at me. Her smile is meltingly hot. "Me and Dan, it's just a contract. We never, you know... There has never been anything between us."

"Okay." For someone who can be so eloquent, she's really saying a lot while saying nothing at all today.

"To answer your question from before. We're not together. No matter what it looks like, you need to trust me."

I smile back. "I do trust you." It's a lie. This little piece of me will always believe that she has to want my brother more.

I don't trust my brother with Penny — especially if he finds out I like her — but I *want* so much to trust her. I need to believe that there's a chance.

# Chapter Ten

*Penny*

Making out with Pace is not part of the don't-meet-a-guy plan. After our near-miss kiss, we track down the others and spend the rest of the day with them. Even Emma and her beau decide to join us. If it wasn't for the tagalong fans, the bodyguard and the fact that Karl sees every ride as an opportunity to take more photos of me and Dan, it would have been a totally fun day out.

"Did you have a nice time?" asks Terri, as I step through the door.

"Lovely. It was a bit hot, but the park was amazing." Dan grabs my hips and walks me through to the entryway, allowing everybody else to come in.

"It was great," he adds, kissing my neck. "Penny was beautiful. Karl took loads of photos. I'll show you later."

Gus runs over to us and tries to climb up my leg. "Hey, you, did you miss us?" He gets over-excited, and jumps up and down, asking to be picked up. I hoist him up into my arms and get dog-kissed to death. "We brought you a present. Do you want to see it?" I'd insisted that we stop off at the pet store. This poor doggy has no toys, and he's slowly destroying everything in Pace's room.

"Your little guy missed you," says Terri. *My dog. What a laugh.* I've dreamed of this moment all my life — the fiancé, the puppy, the family. Now I have it all. Except, of course, I don't.

Pace walks in through the door, loaded down with bags, and Gus goes crazy. Yeah. This puppy knows who his dad is, and it's not Dan.

"Hey, buddy." Without thinking, Pacey puts down the bags and steps up behind me, placing a hand on my back and leaning in to snuggle with Gus. We'd make the perfect little family if it weren't for the fact that I'm supposed to be engaged to his brother. I nudge him in the ribs with my elbow and give him the look. The *'don't touch me in front of your parents'* look.

He lets out a pained sigh and takes Gus out of my arms, giving him the biggest hug.

The hallway is getting crowded, and everybody grabs their stuff and heads off to their respective rooms. We all agreed that everyone was going to have dinner in their rooms tonight. Terri and Bob are off, out to a restaurant, courtesy of Dan, and Emma is out with her new boyfriend.

Dan waits until the coast is clear then he sneaks off with Kelli. Those two can't keep their hands off each other. Every opportunity they got today they were fondling each other's butts. It would be cute if Dan hadn't spent every public moment with his arms wrapped around me. I traipse upstairs and head for the shower. God, it's going to be good to get washed and into my pajamas.

I'm secretly hoping that Pace will be on the balcony tonight. I know I shouldn't, and I know if Kelli ever finds out she'll have my guts for garters, but I want to be alone with him again, looking out at the sea, talking about books and movies until we can't resist sleep anymore.

Avoiding kissing those sweet, sweet lips shouldn't be an issue. We were, after all, able to stop ourselves from falling into each other's arms as we huddled together for warmth. At least I know now how he feels about me. He was *very* pleased to be so close.

As the warm water runs down my soapy skin, I slide my hand between my legs. Pace is the only thing on my mind. Yesterday, watching the sweat dripping down his body as he pulled that rope was like nothing I've ever seen before. It was a cascade of deliciousness.

Nobody should legally be allowed to look that sexy in public.

The touch of his hands, the sound of his voice, the way his eyes eat me up every time he looks at me seeps into my mind, and I imagine him standing right there in front of me. As I bring myself closer to the edge, I can taste his lips on mine. It's almost like he's here in the shower, running his tongue from the crux of my neck and down between my breasts, his hard cock entering me, lifting me, pounding into my eager, wet pussy. Gripping his hands tightly onto my butt, my legs wrapped around him as he makes love to me, firm and hard and unrelentless. I gasp with pleasure.

"Fuck me," I whisper. It's hot, *real*. I lean back against the cold tiles, moaning as the fantasy of him banging me against this very wall brings me to orgasm, my hips swirling to the rhythm of his invisible thrust. "Pacey!" *Oh no. Oh no, no, no.* I come to my senses, so lost in my illusion that I forgot for a moment that I'm not alone in this house.

Pace knocks on the balcony door. "Penny, are you okay? I was laying the table on the balcony and I thought I heard you call my name."

"Yes, sorry, I...uh... I'm in the shower."

He runs into the bedroom, but stops short of entering the en suite. "Did you fall? Are you sure you're okay?" *Fuck, fuck, fuck.* My brain freezes up and I can find no excuse for what I just did other than, well, what I just did. "Are you alone in there?"

*Oh God,* is he planning to join me? I am not ready. Well, I am, but no. That would be a terrible idea. Nothing he could do would live up to what I just imagined him doing.

"Yes. I'm fine. I just... Please, I was just..." *Wanking? Playing with myself while I imagined us fucking?*

"Oh." He chuckles. "Oh my God. Right. Oh shit, I'm so sorry. I was on the balcony and I heard... Oh my God. I'm so sorry. I'm going now. *Fuck,* sorry."

*Great. Awesome. Fantastic.* Now he knows I get off on just the idea of him. I can never leave this room again. I'm just going to stay in this shower until the end of the week. I'll get Dan to deliver my meals here because Pacey is going to tell him and his whole family how I rubbed one off and called out his name.

Conceding that the shower is not going to be my final resting place, I dry myself off and step out, grabbing my pajamas. Pacey is still outside setting up for dinner.

*What was I thinking?* The humiliation.

"Please don't tell anybody."

He turns and looks at me, his very cheeky grin turning serious for just a second before he goes back to giggling.

"That you got shampoo in your eyes and called out for help? Your secret's safe with me." I can't tell if he's being serious. Does he really think that? Did I really get away with it?

"Thank you."

"Are you up for poker and cocktails tonight?" The awkwardness goes down a notch.

I've been thinking about it all day, waiting to be alone with him. "Yes, I'd love to."

"Strip poker this time? It'll give you some more fodder for your spank bank." Oh my God. *Seriously?*

I cross my arms, and stomp my foot. "I hate you."

"That's not what you —"

"Stop. Pacey, no." The cheek of it. "We will never talk of this again. Do you understand me?"

He grins at me and goes back to laying the table. "My lips are sealed."

"Promise?"

"You have to trust me, too, you know," he replies, taking on a more serious tone. "It works both ways. Now, go get your food. Gus will never speak to me again if I don't invite his favorite person to sit and eat with us."

This definitely feels way more relationship-ish than it should, but I push that to the back of my mind. I store it for three a.m. when every other thing that happened today comes back to haunt me.

Just good friends. We haven't even kissed. I can do this, can't I? Sure.

Just good friends.

# Chapter Eleven

*Day Four*
*Penny*

I wake to find someone is spooning me...in my bed.
*There's a man. In my bed. Spooning me.*

I know I had several of those very delicious tequila cocktails last night, but I'm pretty sure I went to bed alone. "What the f—?"

A gruff voice whispers in my ear, "Don't panic."

*What?* "Huh?"

"Act normal. Parents incoming."

I open my eyes, pull up the sheet that is barely covering my naked body and turn my head a little. The stench of stale cigarettes and vodka hits my nose. "Dan?"

"You overslept, it's eight-thirty a.m. and we're supposed to be meeting up in the dining room before going out for the day." I reach a hand behind me and gently touch his leg. "Don't worry. I'm not naked. I just... My mom's about to come in in three...two... one."

"Dan, Penny? Oh no, did we wake you? I'm so sorry." She pops her cheery face through the curtains, and I pull the sheet over my body some more, as if it could make me less naked. "I was just saying to my husband that we should have booked the car for later. We're on vacation. Nobody should be up at this time in the morning when you're on vacation."

"No, it's fine, Mom. We were just getting up." Dan rolls back and sits up. He wasn't lying. He's dressed enough to be decent.

"Good morning, Tuppence!" says Pace, with a sly grin.

Oh no. Just how drunk was I last night? It's all coming back to me. At some point after the third cocktail, we played truth or dare, and I told him my real name. He found it 'cute' and 'unique', but let's be honest. I'm named after a coin. It's never not going to be funny to everybody who hears it for the first time.

Pace's face peers through from behind his mother's then drops his jaw when he sees who I'm in bed with...naked. I want to scream that it's not what it looks like, but it's written in a stupid contract that I can't do that. I'm legally obliged to pretend that I spent the night making love to this man. *Ugh.* That document was airtight. I read it through again yesterday, and there's no getting out of it. Only three days to go and I can return to being officially single, at home, being told off by my best friend for my ridiculous behavior.

"Good morning, Pacey."

I turn to look at Dan, and the grin on my face grows even wider. I can at least console myself in the very awesome fact that their mom named them Pacey and

Dawson and that will always be more amusing than my name. Emma must be thanking the good Lord every day that *Dawson's Creek* was canceled just before she was born. Not many Josephines around these days.

"Let's leave these lovebirds to get ready," says his mum, pushing her inquisitive son back and out of sight.

Why do I care so much what he thinks, anyway? I did my due diligence and made sure he understood exactly where I stand when it comes to relationships. No more flirting. Just good friends and all that. His upset face and the little twinge my heart did when I saw it is of no consequence.

I am *not* falling for Pacey Scott.

\* \* \* \*

Okay, truth be told, I may be falling for Pacey Scott. I was doing really well until he walked out of the house looking like an absolute dream.

When Pace dresses up, his demeanor instantly changes. His hidden powers of adultness seep out and he rocks the confident grown-man look.

Today is no exception.

Strolling out of the house looking like he totally owns it, he seems like he could conquer the world — and me with it. In fact, he's conquering my panties right now. I close my mouth and pick imaginary fluff off of my cotton summer dress.

No man has ever looked sexier in cargo shorts, a crisp blue shirt and a backwards cap. What is it about American frat boys and backwards caps? I'm going to be honest. It does things to my insides that are probably illegal in southern Spain. They're very religious here, and my mind is imagining all the things I would do with that man and his starched shirts.

He glances over nonchalantly, catching me gaping. He winks at me salaciously. *Fuck him*, I swear he doing it on purpose. The incident in the shower yesterday has boosted his confidence. He knows he has me, and he knows I can do nothing about it.

I could really do with not falling in love with Pacey Scott.

The driver takes us to a ferry where we take a private boat that whisks us over to another island. There are live volcanoes on Isla del Fuego — hot, bubbling molten-lava-type volcanoes. Apparently we're heading for a restaurant where they grill food with the aforementioned fiery liquid rock.

I'm looking forward to it. It's nice to get out and away from the pressure of the house and of keeping up appearances all the time.

Dan is fast asleep next to me, his head back, gentle snores coming from his mouth. He is devastatingly handsome, I'll give him that. Even after a night of debauchery with several other people, he still looks like a Greek god.

I peer over at Pace, who hasn't spoken to me since our gazes crossed in my bedroom this morning. Is he hurting? Is he sad about what he thinks he saw?

The record needs to be set straight. It's not that, you know, I need him to think that I'm still available or anything. I just need him to know that I didn't lie. I'm not a lying liar who says one thing and does another…or his brother. He needs to know that I didn't do his brother. I need to get him alone to set things straight.

The driver parks and we are informed that there is a short bus tour which will take us to the restaurant. Everybody else is piling on to public, shared coaches, but it appears we have a small bus all to ourselves. I don't like to think about how much all this costs. Contrary to popular opinion, I don't have a huge amount of disposable income. Well, I do, but it's tied up in investments and foundations and things like that. I certainly wouldn't be spending it on the extravagance of doing everything privately. I know Dan is famous, but he's not that famous, right? He can mingle a little with commoners. They're not going to bite.

We get out of the car to stretch, the heat of the morning hitting us as we step outside. This place is roasting — and not just because of the volcanoes. I grab my sunscreen and slather on a third coat. I'm not taking any risks. Nobody wants to discover what burned Penny looks like. It's not a pretty sight.

"Looking forward to seeing the volcanoes?" asks Terri as we're ushered onto our luxurious bus. "Come sit with me so we can talk weddings."

I look over at Dan, who has already found a seat and mysteriously, immediately fallen straight back asleep again. It's the only way of avoiding speaking to his parents, isn't it? *Sneaky buggar.*

"Sure." Terri and I sit down at the front of the bus because *'they're the safest seats'* and she grills me for a good half an hour about churches and flowers and bridesmaids and how we can't have Dan's cousin because she gets mouthy after a couple of drinks and she almost ruined her mother's twenty-fifth wedding anniversary. This is then followed by a long and detailed description of Dan's family — who's married to who, how Dan is just like his grandfather and how he's going to be the best father. She doesn't mention Emma or Pacey once. This woman is blinkered when it comes to her kids. It breaks my heart. I didn't have great parents. I always knew, to some degree, that they loved me, but they just didn't know how to cope with me or care for me.

Terri, though, she has everything—a wealthy husband, a good home, a large family. She should be getting it right, but she's getting it spectacularly wrong. Even her favorite son lies to her. One day it's all going to come crashing down, and she's going to wonder what hit her. Emma and Pacey are going to give up trying to please her, and she's going to wake up to the fact that *her* Dan, sweet though he is, is never going to be the perfect son she so desires.

As the bus draws up at the restaurant, I'm glad to escape the suffocating negativity of this woman. Behind her kindly façade she is cruel, mean and self-serving. The conversation has devolved into her insulting everybody in her family and painting herself as an angel who has to put up with them. The opposite is most definitely true.

We step down and I stand aside, waiting for Pace to get off. I just want to hug him and tell him everything is going to be all right.

"So this is a live volcano, right?" he says, staring down at the brochure we've just been handed. "That's scary."

Was he even listening at dinner last night? Karl explained everything in detail. "I'm sure it's not dangerous, otherwise we wouldn't be able to visit it."

The tour guide starts to drone on about the history of the island and myths and traditions surrounding the volcanoes. Pacey and I stare at the barren landscape.

There's literally nothing but red sandy dunes and dark black rock. It's fascinating and, yet, so desolate. *Ugh.* Terri has brought my mood right down, and I'm pretty sure Pacey's still pissed about the whole '*naked in bed with his brother*' thing.

"It's not what it looked like," I mutter under my breath. "This morning. It wasn't what it looked like."

"You and Dan? Look... You're free to do whatever you want. Why do I care? You've got to get those pent-up frustrations out somehow, right? Do you call out my name or his, though? You know, when you —"

"Seriously? I thought your lips were sealed. I don't want you to think I've been lying about it being" — I look around to make sure nobody's within earshot. They're all at the front of the group pretending to be fascinated by volcanoes — "fake."

"Like I said, I don't care."

*Liar. You do care. I want you to care. I want you to be bothered by it, to be jealous and angry that you weren't that man in my bed.*

"You don't seem like you don't care."

"You're like a sister to me. You said it yourself. And it didn't look like nothing. You were naked, Penny. You weren't wearing a damned thing."

The gasp that comes out of my mouth is way louder than I intend. "You *saw*?"

*Oh God.*

"Penny, everybody saw."

*Fuck. Really?*

He kicks at the dirt, avoiding my gaze, as if the idea of me naked has the same effect on him as the vision of him in a crisp cotton shirt does to me.

"He wasn't there at three a.m., and he wasn't there this morning. I overslept and he was covering for me. Nothing happened."

"Good."

"Good."

I move to the front of the group and loop my arm through Dan's.

*Good. Great. I'm so glad we had this talk.*

# Chapter Twelve

*Penny*

"Are you following me?" I snap. Pace stands there looking as guilty as hell.

"No."

He hasn't spoken to me for the entire day. Lunch was awkward as hell with his mum droning on and on about the wedding, Kelli and Pacey getting more and more jealous and Dan getting more and more frustrated with his mother. Only Emma, who'd dragged the lovesick Jean-François along, was having any fun. Bob, as usual, was hard to read. At a guess, I'd say he was as indifferent about all of this as he seemed to be about everything in his life.

This afternoon we've all been given the option of going to the beach or doing something on our own. I haven't had a moment to myself since I got here, so I've opted for a visit to a local town. Shopping therapy is sometimes the best, and I've got a sizeable fake-girlfriend-contract check burning a hole in my pocket.

"Really? You just happened to get dropped off at the same town as me?"

Pacey tries his best to look pious, but he just looks hot and bothered and totally fed-up. "I wanted to apologize. I didn't mean to be rude. The relationship between you and my brother is none of my business."

"The only relationship your brother and I have is a legally binding one." I pause. "Well, that's not true. He's obviously my friend, too, but that's where we draw the line."

"I don't care."

*Yes, you do.*

I say it for him, if he's going to continue denying it. Yesterday's near-kiss wasn't him not caring. "You do and that's okay, but stop pretending it's anything else." I head toward the town center. "Look… I'm going shopping. You're welcome to join me, but if any of your sentences involve the relationship I have with your brother, I'm out—as in it's over, our friendship."

"Friendship?" he replies, raising an eyebrow.

I nod unconvincingly. "I may have mentioned this before, but just in case it's not clear, I cannot and will not be getting involved with anybody in the near future. Fake contracts aside, I made a promise."

"Sure, and how's that working out for you?" he says, a touch of snark in his voice.

*As well as you can imagine, faced with you.*

We wander down the closed-off street. The main part of town is an eclectic mix of stores. Souvenir shops sit aside high-class boutiques and restaurants. Small stands selling pretty silver jewelry or Spanish delicacies block every available alley or street corner.

I stop at a stand and study the earrings. "So, what's the goal?"

"Huh?"

"You said you were studying medicine. What's your specialty going to be?"

I hand him my purse and he carries it while I hold a pair of earrings up to the side of my face. "I don't know. I'm about to start my second year."

"So, a doctor of some kind." I put the earrings down and smile at the stallholder, moving along to the next stand.

"That's the plan."

I can't imagine anything further from my line of work. DJs don't generally date doctors. It's not that there's any kind of rule. It's just that we don't exactly run in the same circles.

"Have you always wanted to be a doctor?"

Pace hands me back my purse and grabs a couple of free samples of chorizo from a plate. He holds one up to my mouth then pops it in when I open. "My whole life. There's nothing else. I worked so hard to finish high school early because I just wanted to get there, you know?"

"Ooh, get this one. It's spicy." I point to my mouth, trying to chew the delicious, fiery sausage before replying. "Is it true that med students never sleep?"

He grabs his wallet from his pocket and points at the different meats he wants from the stand. "Every weekend I spend every hour when I'm not studying sleeping. I make my bed my home."

"Must not leave much time for a personal life."

He grabs his bag of food then turns to look at me. "Is that some kind of weird way of asking me if I have a girlfriend back home?" I shrug. It's not like I don't have a vested interest. "No. I don't have anything resembling a personal life."

We walk along the high street, dipping into shops and trying all the food, even though we ate more than enough at lunchtime. It's comfortable and easy and nice. You're not supposed to say 'nice'. You're supposed to say 'amazing' and 'incredible', but it's just nice. Pace has this way about him, this serenity that allows me to breathe in his presence. Whether we're playing cards or sitting on the beach or shopping, he doesn't feel the need to challenge or correct me.

Reece always wanted to better me. My career, in terms of the amount of money I've made and the success of my music, was going way better than his. He presented a morning TV show. He didn't write anything, and he didn't have any productive input into the show. He just turned up, read the lines on the monitor and looked pretty. And yet, I was never enough. He'd had bigger better plans for me, and none of them included my happiness. They tended to include fancy hair, pretty nails and high heels. Nothing about me was good enough for that man, and yet I'd so desperately wanted to be his wife. *Why?*

I could count the number of flattering remarks Reece had made during our relationship on the fingers of one hand. Pace has already told me how beautiful I am three times since we started walking down the street.

Well, he didn't say it exactly. He mentioned that the earrings I'd tried on were just perfect for my face, and that any earring would look pretty on me. He'd told me to stop worrying about the amount of cheese I was sampling at the delicatessen because nobody ever wishes they'd eaten less cheese when they reflected on their life. He told me to buy both dresses because both of them looked stunning on me.

Pace is fast becoming one of the most incredible men I've ever met, and yet I'd promised Kelli. I'd sworn to her that I wouldn't fall in love. *How can I not, though? How can I walk away from this beautiful man?*

"Do you want an ice cream?"

I nod. Clearly, today is a day of indulging fantasies and food.

I sit with all our shopping bags while Pace queues. He's such a gentleman. A 'pull out your chair', 'hold a door' kind of man. He constantly refers to women's indifference toward him, but this confuses me. Sure, he dresses like a fifty-year-old man in his shirts and shorts and he's constantly pushing his glasses up his nose, but he's gorgeous and sweet and kind. Maybe I bring something out in him that he doesn't show around other women.

They say there's someone for everyone. Am I the one for him? Did fate throw Dan in my path all of those years ago to lead us here? *No, that's ridiculous.*

I'm getting attached to this guy, and I'm losing control. He lives thousands of miles away. He has no time for me, and he's about to start his second year of med school. Yet it constantly occurs to me that kissing Pace's lips would be really quite delicious, and being loved by him would feel amazing. Us being together would mean betraying his brother in his parents' eyes, and he does not need that kind of stress in his already-very-busy life. It's all opposites and contradictions, and my brain can't cope.

No. Friendship is good. I can do it. I'll calm my desires, take cold showers and try to stop spending all my time with him. I'll pretend that he really is my brother-in-law — out of bounds, forbidden, good buddies.

He walks up to us, hands me a small pot of ice cream then proceeds to give his swirly strawberry cone the most scintillatingly sexy lick I've ever seen in my life. How dexterous is that man's tongue? How long and flexible is it?

I feel the blood draining from me as I have thoughts that no person should be having in a public place. I cross my legs and try to think of something dull and boring.

Pace glances down at me and smiles. He knows exactly what's running through my mind, the cheeky bastard.

He bites his tongue, pauses for a second as he readjusts his cargo shorts then goes in for another lick.

"Spank bank," he whispers, raising an eyebrow.

I take back everything I said.

He's evil. Terribly torturously evil. Not a gentleman at all.

I'm falling in love with Pacey Scott, and this is not good. It's very bad indeed.

* * * *

*Pacey*

We move over toward the beach, find a bench to sit on and enjoy the view. "So what's this whole thing about you trending on Twitter?"

"What?" Penny looks up from her phone.

"When Karl was trying to take those promo photos at lunch, he said to buck up your ideas, otherwise you'd be trending on Twitter again. What did he mean? More importantly, do I need to kick someone's butt?"

She laughs. "No, please don't kick anybody's butt on my behalf, although thank you for the offer. He's referring to my ex-fiancé. Remember that I'm doing all this to get my revenge."

"Oh, yeah. So what happened there?"

She rolls her eyes and looks at me as if she suddenly hates all men.

*Ooh, this is bad.*

"That whiny bastard didn't like the fact that I wasn't all heartbroken about our relationship ending, and he took his revenge."

Whiny bastard? *Wow.* Remind me never to piss off Penny. "You *weren't* heartbroken, then?"

"Of course I was. We were supposed to be getting married, and he walked out on me while we were…um…being intimate, then he cheated on me, then he ghosted me until I went to his house and dumped him…on the day before our wedding. I just didn't let him *know* that I was heartbroken. I could hardly let a man like that win, could I?"

Penny is honest and real. I have to remind myself that she's managed to keep her identity from the whole world for years. The woman is in so many ways an open book, and yet at the same time, she has all these secrets.

Beautiful as I find her, she hides her body away whenever she can, almost ashamed. Then there's my brother. Her love for him appears to be genuine, but it makes no sense. Dan fucks *everybody*. It just isn't humanly possible that he didn't sleep with Penny. Impossible.

She's so fucking complicated and interesting. I want to know everything.

I rub my shoes on the sandy ground. "So let me get this straight. He walked out on you mid…lovemaking, slept with someone else then just forgot that you were supposed to be getting married."

She closes her eyes, nodding her head at the sheer absurdity of it. "Yup. Then I met you guys."

"When?"

She bites her lip. "Uh…the next day."

In the airport? She was hungover because it was supposed to be her fucking wedding day. *What?* No way should she have been making business deals with my brother. She was hardly even in a fit state to fly. I can't believe he even considered making her do that. I'm going to need a minute here.

I can't hide my shock and disgust. "Holy fuck, Penny. Your wedding day. You shouldn't have been signing contracts. Dan was way out of order."

"Yes, but, you know, it wasn't like that. It was a quickie registry office wedding — I think you guys call it a town-hall wedding — not a big fancy to-do with the whole family and all the tra-la-la that goes with it. Reece didn't want any fuss."

He didn't want anything at all. He wanted to get into her pants then fuck off when it suited him.

I take my glasses off and rub them on my T-shirt as I try to find something more intelligent to say. "I'm just… I can't."

"It was over long before all that happened. I didn't see that everything was falling apart. So blinded was I by my desire to get married that I didn't even realize he was walking away until it was too late. It's all my fault. Kelli calls it 'ring fever'. She says I come down with it every time I date someone. She's not wrong. I do have a tendency to get engaged."

"You're twenty-one? How many times have you said yes?"

She bites her lip again. It's going to be red raw by the end of this conversation. "Three times."

"Three!" It comes out way louder and far more brusque than I'd intended and she leans back a little. "Sorry… I didn't mean to shout. I don't get it. How can you have had time in your adult life to be engaged *three* times?"

Was one of them with my brother? *Please, Lord, don't let her tell me she was engaged to my brother.*

She starts to count her fingers. "Once when I was sixteen. That relationship lasted three months in total, including the proposal. I was saving myself for marriage but he wasn't—at least, not with me."

So, basically, right from the start she was getting screwed over by the men in her life. Noted. "Okay."

"Then, when I was eighteen my second boyfriend proposed, or, well, he wanted us to move in together and I said that I didn't want to live with him if he didn't want to marry me, so he said we could get married."

He doesn't sound as bad as everybody else she'd dated, but I don't want to think about how it ended. "And why didn't you marry him?"

She scrunches up her nose. "He didn't want children. I mean, not many people want kids at eighteen, but he didn't want kids ever."

"You wanted kids straight away?"

She smiles wistfully. "No…just at some point. I couldn't imagine my life without kids. We're still friends, though. That one actually worked out okay."

Oh thank God. "Then you finally got one to agree to be dragged down the altar…well, almost."

"You're hilarious. And obviously not." She scowls. "So I promised Kelli I wouldn't date anybody for at least six months, although she's hoping I can make it a year."

It's not like she hasn't mentioned that at least a hundred times in my presence. As if it's not me she has to convince.

"No sex for a year?" Breaks my heart.

"No. I said I wouldn't date anybody. It's 2021, and you can sleep with people now outside of marriage — or so they tell me."

"You realize that the fake engagement with Dan counts, right? That makes four. Should I be worried? Are you going to come at me with a ring and a dress when I least expect it?"

She giggles. "Serial wedder? I have a bouquet and I'm not afraid to use it…"

"Don't go down the aisle…"

"And whatever you do, don't lift the veil…"

I lean my head on her shoulder. She smells so good, like honeysuckle on a spring day, and I pause for a second to just breathe her in. "So backtracking to the whole sleeping around thing."

She shoves me off. "I didn't say sleeping around. I said I wasn't dating."

"But you're planning to have sex at some point — with a man, no strings."

"Yes. Why? Are you offering your services?"

*Yes. Yes I'm offering my services. Fuck it. How can I make it any clearer?*

"Are you kidding? And wake up in a suit with a flower in my buttonhole and a church filled with my closest friends and family? I'm not falling for it that easily...Bridezilla."

*Damn it. Damn me and my good conscience and my desire to be good.*

She throws me a cheeky smile. "Shame."

"What?" This is the most frustrating conversation I've ever had with anybody in my life. Just kiss me or tell me you want to sleep with me or do something to help me understand where I stand here.

"It's a shame that you're not falling for my evil bridezilla ways."

*Fine. Don't then.* "Yeah. It's a damn shame."

# Chapter Thirteen

*Penny*

Kelli curls a twist of my hair around the curling iron. "Four people?" I say into the mirror in front of us.

Dan suddenly announced this morning that he is holding a party tonight. He's befriended several of our neighbors and they are all coming around tonight for a little soirée. Good music, good food and most likely good sex to follow — well for some of his guests anyway. From the sounds of it, most of them will be in bed with him and Kelli.

"Yes."

"In one bed."

"Uh-huh." She looks amazingly chill for someone who spent the whole night frolicking with strangers — and more awake than I imagine I'd be if I'd had the week she's had so far. She and Dan have not taken a night off from their sexual shenanigans since they got here.

"How does that even work? I mean, do you like pick one and do whatever you want with them then, after a while, you swap? Do you kiss the girls? Does Dan mind if you sleep with another man?"

She laughs and waves her hand dismissively, as if everybody knows the answers to these types of question. I honestly don't know how these things work. I've heard about ménages à trois, but I've never done one. One penis and no lady-parts — well, except my own — is about all I can handle.

"If this is blowing your mind, we don't have to talk about it. We can talk about how you've almost kissed Pacey like a million times but you haven't, because you really like him and you promised me that you wouldn't date someone serious."

*Ugh.* I'd rather not. I'd rather stay here in the comforting hands of my best friend and not think about how every time I get near that man I just want to rip his clothes off and ravage him. Just the idea gives me a little flicker downstairs. This whole 'being friends' thing is a crock of shit. I want him... *now.*

"No. Your sexploits are good. We don't have to discuss anything involving me and my disastrous love life — or lack of love life."

She smiles condescendingly. "You know why I made you promise?"

I nod, like the good, well-behaved girl that I am. "Because I always fall in love and get my heart broken."

"Exactly. And what's going to happen at the end of the holiday? Pacey is going to go back to the US, and you are either going to go home and cry into your pillow or you are going to follow him, and it's going to be a disaster because you're going to want to get married to—"

"Maybe he'll *want* to marry me."

Kelli stops what she is doing, puts the curling iron down and sinks onto the dressing table, directly in front of my face. "Tell me I didn't hear you say what I thought I heard you say."

*Gulp.* "I'm not saying I'm going to marry him. I'm just saying that it isn't out of the realms of possibility." I could marry him, eventually, if I moved to America. It's not a ridiculous idea.

She leans right in so our noses are touching. "Am I going to have to whip some best-friend ass?"

I shake my head really slowly. "No."

"Is Pacey going to marry you?"

Still shaking my head. "No."

*Is it so bad that I have my fingers crossed behind my back?*

She leaps back up and grabs another hunk of hair. "Good. Now promise me that you won't kiss that boy tonight, even though you look like a fucking goddess. There are plenty of gorgeous rich men out there who will be more than happy to kiss you. Pick anyone but him, okay?"

I give her my sweetest smile. *Sure, why not? Plenty of fish in the sea. Just don't kiss Pacey. Got it.*

* * * *

I open the door. "What do you think?"

"Fuck, you look amazing." Pace's eyes pop right out of his head. I am indeed 'a fucking goddess'.

Somehow Dan has roped me into doing a set at the beginning of the evening. That's not going to be easy in the tight-fitting, slinky little red number I chose for tonight. I don't normally get dressed up when I work, but we've all been informed that it is strictly a black-tie, cocktail-dress kind of party. Ironic, really, because I don't think I've ever seen Dan in a suit—well, not off screen, anyway. I doubt that he'll stray far from the black jeans and Henley shirts that adorn his body at all times. Well, when he isn't in those damn short red shorts.

Pace, however, is a man made for a shirt and tie—and he isn't disappointing tonight.

"You don't look so bad yourself." He doesn't just look hot. He looks 'rip my clothes off, dive onto the bed, beg you to fuck me' hot.

He tugs at his shirtsleeves in a sexy way and straightens his collar for effect. "Thank you."

I point to our little table where we play cards and drink cocktails every night. "I stole some champagne. Fancy a drink before we have to go down and talk to rich people who won't like us?"

He chuckles. "Okay. Why won't they like *you*, though?"

It baffles me that he totally accepts the fact that they won't like him. Rich women love hot doctors in suits. He's going to go down a treat.

"I'm just the DJ. For the people downstairs, it's akin to being a member of staff. Not that that's bad… You know what I mean. Plus, they all think I'm sleeping with the host, which, you know, kind of makes it weird. I'm the competition and the help, all at the same time."

"I get it. I'm hoping to meet someone who's looking for someone who isn't going to be free to date for another six years or so."

My stomach sinks as the words come out of his mouth. It looks like he has finally accepted my rebuffs. Whatever we've been building up to or hedging for the last few days is now officially no longer on the cards. He deserves to be happy.

I muster a weak smile. "They'll be lining up."

He strolls out and heads over to the table, serving us both a flute of champagne. We sit down and clink our glasses together.

"Here's to being terribly unsociable."

Pace raises an eyebrow and leans in closer. "Can I ask you a personal question?" he says, lowering his voice.

"Maybe. That depends what it is."

"Why do you do everything he asks? Like being the DJ at a party where you're supposed to be hanging off his arm tonight."

I hold my breath in, not wanting to say something I shouldn't. "I don't do every—"

"You literally agreed to pretend to be his fiancée. You've let him kiss and hug you for the last week. You let him climb into bed with you when you were naked." He raises an eyebrow because he knows he's right. I know he's right, too, but it's still not my business to say.

"In my defense, I woke up like that."

He shakes his head in disbelief. "But you didn't kick him out. *Why*?" The last word comes out so painfully, as if it physically hurts him to think about the fact that I didn't reject his brother, that I'm willing to be so close to Dan and do everything for him.

My heart tightens at the idea that I'm putting Pace through this. I want to tell him. I really do.

"You're not going to let it drop, are you?" All week Pace has been needling at me, slowly and surely, trying to get the story of how I know his brother out of me. "It's not my story to share. Well, my side is, but not his and if I tell you mine, I have to tell you his."

"Babe?" Dan pops his head out of the window. "Can you do my tie for me?"

"Speak of the devil…" I say, getting up and fixing Dan's tie. "Your brother wants to know how we met." Dan gulps hard, his Adam's apple pushing at my hands as he lifts his head and allows me to fiddle with his collar. "I said it wasn't my story to tell," I add, giving him a reassuring smile.

"Tell him," says Dan, looking over at Pace. "Brothers shouldn't have secrets."

*Wow, okay.* Normally I'm sworn to secrecy. "You sure?"

He nods and pecks me on the forehead, still looking at Pace. "Yeah."

I place my hands on his cheeks and bring his face down to mine. "Love you."

"Love you, too," he replies, then kisses me on the nose, and takes his leave.

"Love you, too-o," says Pace sarcastically, raising his glass.

I grab my glass and serve myself a second glass of bubbly. "Your brother and I met when we were sixteen. I was in the US with my manager, working on my first album. Dan was working on his first movie. We crossed each other's paths all summer. I was dating him at the time—my manager, I mean, not Dan. And my manager was close friends with Dan's co-star and girlfriend."

"Wait, what?"

"Yeah. Twenty-one-year-old me wants to go back and slap sixteen-year-old me around the head for thinking that it was okay to fall in love with a guy in his late twenties who promises you the world. In my defense—and I guess in his—we never slept together."

"He's the first engagement. The guy who cheated?"

"Yes, I'm getting to that. Dan fell in love, too—like the deep, heartfelt, soul-crushing first love that consumes you. He was working ninety percent of the time and partying the other ten percent. His every moment was spent with this girl. He never went home, never slept, never had anybody to ground him, to notice that he was burning out."

"What? My mom is constantly on his back."

"Not in the way that you think she is. Back then, she was juggling running a home—or at least dealing with the staff—supporting a husband with a successful business, a son who was graduating high school and a turbulent daughter. Now she's living the life she always wanted—a socialite with no responsibilities. She has time to make sure he's successful and well-liked. It's in her best interest to do so. Back then? Well, she just made sure he brought in the cash."

I explain how I got a call from Dan one night, telling me that he'd found my boyfriend in bed with his girl. I'd gotten all fired up, been ready to go and kick some boyfriend ass, but then I'd had the strangest feeling that I should be more concerned about the guy on the other end of the phone.

"So you never confronted your boyfriend?"

"No. I went to Dan's place instead. I…" I hesitate. He'd said I could talk about it, but just how much did he want his brother to know? "I saved his life, Pace. I stopped him from doing a very bad thing then I stayed with him for days. I switched off our phones and closed the curtains and allowed him to grieve and to heal. We disappeared. We talked and we slept and we ate junk food and watched old movies on TV."

"Saved his life?" He squints at me. "What does that—?"

125

"He had a gun."

Pace sits back into his chair and just stares at me, aghast. "What are you talking about? Dan? No! No, he wouldn't..." I shrug, for lack of words to describe the reality of the situation. I'm pretty sure not a single person in this household knows how deeply depressed Dan was at the time, how easy it would have been for him to end it all. "I had no idea. He's my twin, and I had no idea."

"Sometimes all people see is Dan Scott and not Dawson Scott, the man behind the face. I think you forgot to see your brother, and the more you saw him as Dan, the further you grew apart."

Visibly upset by this, Pace just sits there, contemplating my words. He's fighting it, but a tear slides down his cheek, then another. "Fuck. Why didn't he call *me*?"

"He didn't even call me, not really. I just kind of knew, from his voice. It's not really something people like to talk about, you know? There's a stigma to it, a certain shame. I've never told anybody this story before. I've always respected his privacy. Our secret. Well, his therapist probably knows about it, too."

I can see Pace's mind whirring. Little pieces of his life clicking into place.

"Thank you," he mutters, still shocked by what he's heard. "Thank you."

Leaning over him, I wipe the tears from his cheeks with my thumb. "Any time." I down the rest of my glass and clunk it down on the table. "Shall we?"

He stands up, loops my arm through his and leads me down the stairs, all the time looking at me in a whole new way. "I think I might have to love you, too, Penny Farthing."

"I'd like that very much," I reply as we enter the room and I walk over to his brother, slipping back into the role of his fiancée. *Very much indeed.*

# Chapter Fourteen

*Penny*

I pick up my phone to continue the text conversation with Kelli, who has already disappeared with Dan. This has to be the worst party ever. Seriously, if I'd known how dull it would be, I would have done my set then left. As it is, I've chatted with over a dozen creepy guys with wandering hands and eyes, and I haven't met a single person who even comes close to being as incredible as Pace.

Plus, the women here are beautiful...like *expensive* beautiful. I'm pretty sure Dan invited every model in the vicinity just to make me feel short.

*Ugh. Everybody here is so fucking gorgeous. I feel so awkward and unpretty.*

I send the text, knowing full well that she's probably participating in her hundredth orgy of the week and is far more interested in tits and bums than chatting with me.

I survey the room and Pace catches my eye. He's surrounded by gorgeous models, all fawning and fussing over him. That shirt really is perfectly handsome. He's got a bit of a tan since we got here, too. All those mornings sitting on the balcony and walking Gus... Plus, tonight he opted to forego his glasses, which means he really *does* look like his brother. He grabs his phone from his back pocket. Looks down at it then back up at me, his mouth agape.

My phone pings.

*What the fuck, Tuppence?*

What? Kelli never calls me by my name. Oh no. *Shit, shit, shit.*

I'd texted Pace.

I try to reply but my hands are all shaky. *Fuck.* He must think I'm such an idiot.

A hand swoops in as I'm typing and wraps itself around my fingers. He pulls me through the crowd and out onto the balcony. The cool night breeze hits us as we step outside. We're the only ones out there. He slams the door shut as he goes.

"I'm—"

"No." He doesn't let me finish. Wrapping his big warm hands around my cheeks, he stands over me, staring into my eyes, a furious scowl on his face. Is he mad at me? My heart is beating right out of my chest, I've never seen him so fired up. "Don't let me *ever* hear you say you're not pretty. You are beautiful—more beautiful than any of those women."

"If I'm so beautiful, why don't you want me?"

"I've wanted you since the first time I laid eyes on you, but I couldn't do a damn thing about it." He takes in a long, slow breath, licks his lips with the very tip of his tongue. "I'm going to kiss you now. May I kiss you?"

I give him the slightest nod, but he can already see it in my eyes. He can feel the electricity that's running through us as he holds my head in his. He knows I want him as much as he clearly wants me.

He drops his lips onto mine, first soft and gentle, then hard and lustful. We stumble back against the wall, hidden from the window. I grab at his shirt, untucking it, eager to grasp his bare skin. I slide my hands onto his back, pulling him against me. He gasps through his kiss. Has he dreamed about it like I have? Has he imagined what it would be like to kiss like this, to savor the touch of each other's bodies?

He releases from me, his lips hovering over mine.

"Can we take this somewhere else? Somewhere private?" I ask, gripping onto his sides with the tips of my fingers, holding him as close to me as he can possibly be. I don't want to let him go. I don't want to go back into that room with all those gorgeous women and lose him to them again. I don't want to pretend to be Dan's girlfriend anymore. I want none of it.

"We can't go to our rooms. Someone might see."

"What about the beach?" I bite my lip. Are we going to fuck? Is that what's happening right now. I mean, I'm ready for it, but wow, that moved quickly.

He lifts his lips into a wide grin. "Okay." Once again he grabs my hand and leads me off of the balcony and down the steps toward the beach.

"Are we really doing this?"

He turns back, his face a picture of concern. "You don't want to?"

"Oh, I do. I, uh, I just didn't think this was ever going to happen."

I was even looking at other men, thinking for some reason that *any* man would do. That was never the case. I'm not that kind of girl. I fall in love. It's my thing, and Kelli is just going to have to get over it.

"Me neither. I've spent the whole week convinced you were into my brother, but after what you told me tonight, I realize that I've been a complete jerk."

"Oh, you have." He looks back at me and smiles. "But I'm to blame, too. I've pushed you away every single time you got close."

We reach the row of loungers and day beds, deserted at this time of night. It's too early for the party to be making it down to the beach. The sun has barely set.

I sit down on a bed and he lets go of my hand and grabs the drapes surrounding it, unclipping them one by one, giving us all the privacy we need.

He sits next to me on the bed, slips off his shoes then lies down, getting comfortable. "What's so special about me?"

"Huh?" I drop my shoes on the floor, grab a towel, wipe the sand from my feet and join him.

"Why did you have to resist me so?"

"You mean the man who's in med school living his dream, even though it means having literally no social life? The man who lets me beat him at poker every night?" He raises an eyebrow. "Oh, don't deny it. We all know I'm terrible at the game. You're the man who has spent the entire week looking after a puppy that isn't even yours and being adorably cute at it in the process. The man who makes glasses and a buttoned-up shirt so sexy that all I can think about is how much I want to jump him. I can't even believe I resisted you this long."

He grins, his smile taking up most of his face and takes a deep, long breath, as if it's the first one today. Then he snakes his arm around my waist and pulls me backward into a sensual spoon.

He nudges my hair out of the way with his nose, taking the time to breathe in my scent, then whispers, "Do you want that man?"

His dick is pressing into the base of my spine.

*Fuck.*

He slides his hand up my thigh, pushing up my dress. I'll find out soon enough.

He pauses as he reaches the gusset of my thong. "Are you comfortable with this, or do you want me to stop?" he whispers in my ear.

"No. I mean…don't stop. I'm *very* comfortable with this."

"Good." He takes my hand and guides my fingers under the lacy fabric of my underwear and onto my clit. Putting a little pressure on my fingers, he slides them over my already wet pussy and sinks them into me. I let out a little gasp. "Show me how you like it."

I've never done anything like this before. No man ever wanted to know how I like it.

They thought they already knew.

I place my fingers over my clit and swirl them around, his hand is over mine, giving just enough pressure to make it feel like he's doing all the work. Together we bring me to the edge. Sometimes it's just his fingers fucking me as I rub myself, sometimes when he's concentrating on my clit, I enter myself, searching for that all-elusive G-spot that I've yet to find.

My gasps are followed by his moans. He's so into this, so turned on by making me come. The climax builds inside of me. I thrust his fingers deep into my pussy, and I concentrate on my clit. He fingers me so well, so rhythmically that I can almost picture what making love to him must be like as my body shakes and stiffens at our touch.

I lean my head back against his chest, and he lowers his mouth onto mine, devouring my pleasured moans, embracing me as I come.

"Do you have protection?" I ask, as I gather my faculties.

He cringes. "A condom? Oh crap." He reaches into his pocket, pulls out his wallet and looks around in it. "I do. Hey" — he giggles — "you finally got someone to say 'I do'."

"Really?" I reply, unzipping him and slipping my fingers around his bare cock. "You thought that this was the right moment to go for the bridezilla joke?"

He winks at me and pecks me on the lips. "It's always the right time for bridezilla jokes when I'm with you." He struggles to rip open the packet. "You sure you want to? There's no rush. We can take our time."

I bite my lip. "I'm sure."

"Oh, thank God, because I totally — "

"What the fuck?" The curtain opens and Emma stands there, her hand on her hip, trying to stay upright. She's clearly very drunk. "What are you doing with my brother?"

Pace rolls off the bed and faceplants into the sand so that his sister doesn't see, well, *everything*.

She knows exactly what I'm doing with her brother, and there's no need to reply. "Just fooling around with my fiancé," I say. Just how drunk *is* she?

"That's Pace." *Shit.* Not drunk enough.

Pace climbs up onto the bed, fully zipped up — or as well as he can be with a stinking great boner — and wraps a protective arm around me, pulling down my skirt and holding me to him. "Fuck off, Emma. You know she isn't really Dan's girlfriend." My stomach flips. There's something so sexy about my man defending me.

She grabs onto a wooden beam to stabilize herself, and the whole cabana wobbles. "Mom is gonna be so pissed when she finds out you're —"

"Mom isn't going to find out shit, because you're going to shut your mouth." Pace sits up. "I mean it, Em."

"Well, she's on her way down because everyone's looking for you. Gus puked everywhere, and she had to call in a vet. So if you don't want Mom to find out about *her*" — she points at me dismissively — "then you're going to need to get your pants zipped up and get upstairs."

The blood drains from Pace's face. "Gus is sick?"

"Go," I say. "Just go." He pecks me on the head and runs out of there without another word, tucking himself back in as he goes.

"You have no idea the shit you're in. First of all, my mom is going to kill you *and* Dan *and* Pace, and when Dan finds out you're fooling around with Pace, he's going to be super pissed. First rule of this family is that you don't get on Dan's bad side. Every fucker in this place knows that. Dan is the king of my parents' world."

Emma sits down on the bed and falls against me in a big ball of heaving drunken sobs.

"I'm going to need you not to tell anybody about this, not even Kelli," I say. "Can you do that?"

"Fuck you." She is *hammered*. "Nobody cares about me. Jean-François dumped me and nobody cares. It's all 'Dan this' and 'Dan that'."

She gets up, stumbles back down onto the bed then makes it a second time, wandering off toward the sea. I'm going to have to make sure she's all right, aren't I?

I lie back on the pillow. *Fuck*. This is getting complicated. I did not sign up for any of *this*. I close my eyes and lick the sweet taste of Pace from my lips.

Something that feels so good can't be so bad, right? Right.

I hoist myself up. Time to go persuade a drunk teenager that she shouldn't be alone on the beach at night. Fun, fun, fun.

# Chapter Fifteen

*Pace*

I run into the house and follow the heartbreaking sound of a whimpering puppy. My mom is holding him up to her shoulder, rocking him. He looks rough, poor guy. "Where the hell were you?"

*About to have sex with Penny.* "I took a walk on the beach. I'm sorry. Look... He's not even my dog."

"I called your phone."

*I was fingering Dan's fiancée.* "I said I'm sorry."

"Were you with a girl?" I go to take Gus from her arms.

"What does it matter?"

Jesus, it's like the Spanish inquisition. Give me a break.

"Go wash your hands." She has a point. I go into the bathroom and grab the soap.

"He was with a girl," says my mom to my dad, thinking I'm out of earshot. "I hope he used protection." She's rolling her eyes at me. I can feel it.

"One of those models? He should find himself a nice girl like our Dan did." For once I'm in agreement with my father. I found a girl *just* like my brother did.

I walk back into the room and remove Gus from my mother's arms. "How long has he been like this?"

"He started being sick about half an hour ago."

I rub his back and he settles into my shoulder. His whimpers calm down and he starts to snore. "Did you check to see if he ate?"

"No, should I have?"

I sit down on the bed with him and palpate his little belly. I only know how to treat humans, not dogs.

He licks my hand then whimpers again when I push down.

"What the hell did you eat, little dude?"

"Have you got this?" asks my dad, yawning for good measure. It's way past his bedtime and he's clearly eager to get back to sleep.

"Sure. Thanks, guys. Sorry."

My mom rubs my back. "You have responsibilities. You can't be going off with strange women."

*Thanks, Mom.*

"Like I said, Mom, he's not even *my* fucking dog."

"Language, Pacey. Your brother is busy, you know that. It's the least you can do for him after he paid for this holiday for you." She leaves me to it. She takes no responsibility, of course. It *has* to be all my fault.

I say nothing. What's the point? It goes in one ear and out of the other.

It's not like I spend my days studying and working.

I'm twenty-one years old and I'm trying to build a decent future for myself. But sure, I'll just give up the hope of ever having a love life, too, to take care of *Dan's* dog.

"Is he okay?" Penny's voice comes from the balcony.

"I hope so. The vet should be here soon. He probably just ate one too many shoes."

"Can I come in?"

"Sure." She floats through the billowing white curtains like a beautiful angel. "We can't exactly catch up where we left off, though."

She giggles. "I know. Of course not. I just wanted to see if he was okay. I'm kind of attached to the little guy. Don't let him know that, though. He's already got everybody else wrapped around his finger, and his head doesn't need to get any bigger."

"Your secret's safe with me."

"Can I?" She points to the bed and lies down next to me before I have the time to reply. The smell of her perfume hits my nostrils, bringing me right back to where we were only a short while ago. I want to kiss her, but the moment is gone. We're not 'just good friends', but we're not together, either. "You want to know a story?" she asks.

"Uh-huh."

"When I was five, my dad forgot my birthday. It wasn't like I got anything else any other year, but I didn't know about birthdays until then. We had this plastic cake at school, like, it was a piece of Styrofoam that they'd decorated with fake icing and they just changed the candles every time. It was a dusty, dirty old thing but it was the best thing that had ever happened to me. When I got home, I told him, '*You forgot my birthday.*' So he took me down to the pub for once instead of leaving me at home, bought me a Coke and a packet of crisps and somehow he got me a puppy, just like that. It was the best birthday *ever*." She links her fingers through mine and I grab them tight. "I played with it all night, and we took it home and it snuggled up beside me. Then the next day it was gone, and it was no longer my birthday anymore and my dad was no longer behaving like the father he was. He said it ran away, but I know now that he just borrowed it to try to make me smile."

I lift her hand to my lips and place a gentle kiss on her fingers. I never know quite what to say when people say things like that. Nothing I can say or do makes up for her childhood.

"I'm sorry."

"Don't be. I just wanted you to know that if you're feeling like you let this little guy down, you didn't. You're the most amazing dog-dad that this little pup could ever have. You're allowed to have some time for yourself. You're allowed to stop being a med student or the supposedly less-important sibling or puppy-sitter and just have fun being the hot, sexy nerd that you are."

*Hot, sexy nerd? I'll take it…*

She looks up at me and our gazes fix for the longest time. Her eyes light up when she smiles, like little fireworks. I'm totally smitten. She's *fucking* incredible.

This surge builds up inside me, twisting and gripping my gut. *I love her.* Fuck, I really do, I love her. She didn't come here to try to catch up where we left off. She didn't come here with any other goal than to make me feel better because I'd been with her and let Gus get sick. Her intentions are completely unselfish.

And I love her for it.

"Thank you." I take a deep gulp. "I—"

"I should go," she says, interrupting my declaration. "Just in case your parents come back, I don't want to risk it."

"Oh...okay." *No. Stay.* "Yeah, sure, we can't be too careful."

She pecks me on the lips. "Sorry... Were you saying something?"

Gus stirs and starts heaving. I run to the balcony, puppy in my arms, and she follows me outside. "No, nothing. Don't worry," I reply in a whisper, and she leaves from whence she came.

"I love you," I mutter to myself. Gus looks up at me with his big, sad eyes and I'm overwhelmed with guilt for blaming him for interrupting my sexy times with Penny. "It's not your fault, little dude. I love you, too. I'm not that keen when you pee on my stuff and throw up in my room, but I love you, nonetheless."

# Chapter Sixteen

*Penny*

Pace is adorable with Gus. I want to just hug them both and not have to come back here and pretend anymore.

I get back to my room to the sound of sobbing. *Oh dear.* I'd picked up Emma from the bottom of the beach steps and convinced her to haul her arse back to my room, instead of staying out there on her own.

Except, when I step inside, it isn't her who's crying. It's Kelli.

"Oh my God, are you okay?"

She looks up at me, eyes red and swollen, and runs the back of her hand across her nose. "Do I look okay?"

*Fair point.* "No. What's wrong?"

"It's Dan. He brought these girls back to my room, to…uh…" — she looks at Emma and carefully considers what she's about to say — "to…uh…stay overnight, and he asked me to leave. I thought he loved me. I thought

I was the main woman in his life." The last couple of sentences come out with a racked sob between every word.

"Ah, I'm sorry." I don't quite know how to comfort her or even why I should. I warned her about this. I warned her not to get involved, but she refused to believe me. Just as I can't keep my hands off Pace, she just couldn't believe that Dan wouldn't fall in love with her. She has, after all, done everything she can to please him. "If it's any consolation, it's nothing against you. He doesn't mean it. He has...*issues* when it comes to relationships."

"What the hell do you know?" Emma counters, somehow affronted by my stating the obvious. "Dan's my brother. I think I'd know if he had problems."

"Would you?" I reply. It's not fair, I know. Emma is so much younger than her brother. Five years separate them. She hardly knows Dan, because he left home so young. She's not particularly close to her other brother, either. Didn't Pacey mention that she goes to boarding school? "I don't mean to be rude, but I'm actually a lot closer to Dan than both of you might think." Kelli snorts and throws herself back against the headboard. "Not like *that*. We're friends, and I'm telling you that when it comes to love, Dan doesn't always make great decisions. Personally, Kelli, I think you're pretty good for him. You're clearly in love with him, which is a terrible mistake, but whatever. If you want to be with him, and you clearly do, you're going to have to accept that that comes with certain challenges."

"I *do* love him..." Kelli starts to sob again, and I take her into my arms. Loving Dan must be awful. He breaks hearts like French people eat baguettes, on a daily basis, voraciously.

Talking of baguettes. "Are either of you hungry?"

"Huh?" Emma looks up at me and nods, then turns to Kelli. "You should eat. It'll make you feel better."

"Shall we call Chef and ask him if he can send us up a platter or two of leftovers? There must be a ton of food, since nobody at that party was touching it." Kelli thinks about this for a second, then smiles through her tears.

She picks up her phone and starts typing a text. "Do you guys want something to drink?"

"Oh God, I would love a drink." My evening hasn't gone as planned at all. Well, it did veer in the direction of something incredible, but the ending was entirely unsatisfactory. "A couple of bottles of the decent champagne would be nice. And a bottle of Coke for Emma here — and some water."

Kelli laughs. "Chef is going to have to hire a truck to bring all this up to us."

Earlier on, he was boasting loudly about having a whole bunch of minions to do his bidding tonight. He can certainly spare a few to bring us some food.

"Is the party still going?" asks Emma.

"It moved down to the beach about twenty minutes ago," replies Kelli. *Ooh,* it looks like Pace and I left our cabana just in time. That could have been seriously awkward. "Once Dan had gone off for the night, Karl didn't really see the point of having to oversee a bunch of guests, so he just kind of steered them all out and away."

A knock at the door signals our in-house food delivery and a couple of handsome waiters bring platters full of food and drink into the room, much to the delight of the girls. "They're not staying," I say to

Emma as she eyes up one of the guys. "There are enough hormones floating around this house as it is."

I usher the men out of the door before either of them get any ideas. She's not wrong, though. Both of them are drop-dead gorgeous. I'm sure, if they're looking for love, they'll find it on the beach when their shift is over.

"You can talk," she replies. "I don't even want to think about what you were doing with my brother in the cabana."

"Emma," I say through gritted teeth. "My private life is private." I don't need the whole household talking about it.

"So you *are* fucking Dan," adds Kelli with a steely stare. "I knew it."

*Oh crap.* "No, I'm not."

"She's fucking Pace," says Emma with a wicked grin.

"Seriously?" *Jesus.* I hope she doesn't tell anybody else.

Kelli's jaw drops. "What? Oh my God. I need to know everything. I thought you'd decided that you were just going to be good friends. You promised me."

"I'll thank you to change the subject please, ladies. I'm not here to discuss my private life. Mainly because I have an iron-clad contract to fulfill and that means that this discussion is over, understood?"

They nod and giggle between themselves while I open the champagne and hand a glass to Kelli. We tuck into the food and change the subject. Tomorrow's agenda is pretty full again, with a lunch date at a rather exclusive restaurant followed by an afternoon on somebody's private yacht.

Is Pace even going to be there? If Gus is still sick, he might sit this one out. Plus yachts aren't exactly doggy-friendly.

My mind wanders back to the cabana — the touch of his fingers on my body, the musky odor of his aftershave as he rubbed his body against me. If we had the house to ourselves tomorrow, the things we could do.

I'm fucked, though. There's no way Dan — or, rather, Karl — is going to pass up the opportunity to get a photo shoot on the front of the boat, the two of us jumping into the sea, canoodling under the sun.

After tonight, I never want to have to touch Dan again. It was already seriously awkward, but now? Now Pace is going to be watching our every move, judging my every reaction. I signed the contract, I'm a woman of my word, but I am beginning to regret ever thinking that it was a good idea.

Admittedly, if I hadn't bumped into his mum, I wouldn't have seen Dan, and I would never have met Pace. Maybe fate would have thrown him in my path another way. Destiny cannot be so cruel as to make me have to spend another week in the arms of the twin brother of the man I'm falling in love with.

"What you thinking about?" asks Emma.

"Nothing." *Am I blushing?*

"You really like him, don't you?" she asks as she dips a prawn into a spicy red sauce, catching the drips with her hand.

"Don't make a mess, and yes, I do. I'm not the kind of girl who sneaks down to the cabana with just any guy." I wink at her and she giggles.

"I'm glad. He's had a tough couple of years. He deserves someone nice — someone like you."

"Thank you." Emma's support is precious. Plus, it's nice to hear her saying something positive about me. "You're not so bad yourself."

This is exactly what I needed. A girls' night. Moving down to London to be with Reece had meant that Kelli and I could see each other more than a couple of times a month. Hanging out with just my friends is essential to me. I've missed that here.

Sipping on champagne, eating expensive food and chatting about life, the universe and everything, I suddenly find the perfect way to end this very strange evening.

I jump off the bed and rummage around in my suitcase.

"What *are* you doing?" slurs Kelli who has been drowning her sorrows a little too hard.

"I'm getting my dress."

"You brought the dress?" Kelli almost falls off of the bed in shock. "What the fuck? You're kidding me, right?"

"What dress? What's going on?" Emma stares at the both of us in confusion, and she's now the most sober person here.

I hold up my wedding dress. It cost me a fortune but I'm never going to wear it. I could sell it, sure, but it's cursed. Nobody wants to get married in a dress from a canceled wedding. "Who wants to go for a swim?" I grab my bikini, which is drying on the radiator, and start putting it on.

"Now? Have you lost it?"

"Honestly, I feel really great, like I've been liberated from the weight of rejection and uncertainty that was pulling me down." I unzip my party dress and slip it off, grabbing the wedding dress and throwing it on over my bikini. "Well, come on," I say as I head toward the balcony, "Do you want to be my bridesmaids or not?"

They both follow me out, not even bothering to change. Looks like I'm swimming on my own. We run down to the beach, singing the wedding march at the top of our voices. A jump and a leap and I fly into the water. It's cool at this time of night but not cold. The waves push me around as I sit, laughing my head off, soaked from head to toe. This is liberating. It's freeing to just do something so ridiculously pointless, to give the finger to Reece and everybody else who has ever broken my heart.

Kelli runs into the water, still in her beautiful party dress, and Emma follows. The two of them sink down next to me then we jump around in the sea, up to our waists, splashing and giggling.

The lights come on in several houses along the beach and people who are finishing the evening with a quick kiss and a fondle in the dunes come out to see what's going on.

Dan walks out of the ground floor at the same time that his brother walks out of his room. They look at each other then back at us.

In a matter of seconds people are running toward us, and jumping into the sea. Shirts are flying and mobile phones are piling up on the beach as one by one the people around us decide to make this a communal *bain de minuit*.

Jean-François, abashed, wades over to Emma, pulls her into his arms, mutters something romantic, or dirty, or both, to Emma — who looks stunning in her saturated evening-gown — and kisses her passionately. *Looks they're back on.*

Not one to miss out on a party, Dan is in the water and scooping up Kelli before she even knows what's hit her.

I stand there and look at all these loved-up, happy people, laughing and splashing around, and I look up at Pacey, but he's gone, probably dealing with a poorly puppy or the vet—or just back to bed.

"Channeling your inner bridezilla?" says a voice from behind me as he wraps his hands around me and pulls me away from the crowd. "It was just a bit of foreplay, Tuppence Farthing, not a proposal."

"It's a metaphorical, symbolic something or other," I reply, putting my hands under the water and pulling him to me by his shorts.

He plants his lips on mine, forcefully, his tongue exploring me wildly. It's a wanton embrace that has no rhyme or reason, as if he's taking out his frustrations on my mouth.

A bright light shines down on us from above. Terri stands on the balcony, her hands on her hips, unamused by the impromptu beach party only a few yards from her bedroom. I break from the kiss and push Pace down into the water. He swims underneath me, his hands reaching up under my skirt and making me blush under the moonlit sky.

"Stop that noise, immediately. Go on. Get inside, for goodness sake, before somebody gets hurt or drowned!" She crosses her arms and waits for the crowd to disperse.

It appears that the wedding party is over, and it's time for bed.

# Chapter Seventeen

*Day Six*
*Penny*

The morning after is predictably hard for everybody. Even Terri and Bob have difficulty peeling themselves out of bed for the nine a.m. breakfast rendezvous.

Pace mopes in, unshaven and looking a little more like his brother than usual. Normally you can tell the two of them apart straight away, but this morning everybody does a double take.

He gives me a little wink, sending Emma into a fit of giggles. Her hangover is considerably lighter than mine and Kelli's. I'm only a few years older than her, but apparently I'm already ancient.

Gus is looking much chirpier. I heard him whimpering a few times in the night, but he looks like, whatever it was, it's all better now.

"Good morning, everybody," I say, sitting down at the table with a plateful of food. The best cure for a little too much champagne has always been a hearty breakfast, at least where I'm concerned.

Dan is shoveling food down. He ditched the girls from the party after our midnight swim, preferring to take Kelli back to his room instead. He must have built up quite the appetite. He looks up at me and squints, tilting his head to one side. *Crap.* I totally forgot to be all lovey-dovey like I normally am. I grab my plate and go to move but he shakes his head. Too late now.

I shrug and give him the dirtiest look I can muster. I'm not feeling like being besties today, not after last night. I'm kind of pissed with him and his behavior toward my best friend. I know this is what he does, but I don't want him doing it to her.

"Did I do something wrong?" he asks, sticking the knife in a little bit more. *Damn, Daniel. You're supposed to be on my side.*

"Trouble in paradise?" asks his mother, suddenly taking an interest in the conversation.

I shake my head. "Not at all. I wanted to get the lowdown from this guy" — I say, pointing to Karl — "on today's activities."

"She's feeling a bit off today. The seafood," says Emma out of nowhere.

"You do look very peaky," adds Kelli. "Are you worried about the yacht? They can be rocky. Probably not a good idea if you're not feeling very well."

Dan looks at us all as if we've lost it. "She looks fine to me."

"Do you have a fever?" asks his mum, getting up and walking around the table. She slams her hand onto my forehead. "She's very hot."

*I am?* I stick my own palm on my forehead. Feels pretty normal to me. Maybe Terri has cold hands.

"She is," says Pace. "She looks very hot." *Cheeky beggar.* I bite my lip and try to look as peaky as I'm supposed to be feeling.

"It would be a shame if you didn't go on the yacht this afternoon, a terrible missed opportunity," says Karl, with a frown. Not for a second do I believe that Karl has my interests at heart. He wants those paparazzi shots. "But I don't want her near you if she's sick," he adds, shaking his head and looking over at a puzzled Dan. "You're filming the minute we get back to LA. We can't risk you catching anything."

*Squee.* My squad totally has my back.

The conversation moves away from me and on to Dan's new movie. I turn to Kelli. "I see Dan's extra guests are gone this morning."

She grits her teeth and mutters, "Good riddance."

"You're not..." I think about it for a second. The poor girl was in such a state last night. She can't truly believe that he's going to give up his lifestyle and settle down with her, can she? "You're not thinking of staying with him, are you?"

She looks down into her lap. "Maybe? He's my kryptonite."

*Oh good God.* I know I compared him to Superman when I arrived, but the more time I spend with him, the more I'm convinced he's turning into the villain of the story. His love life is certainly a concern, and he is partying as hard as he can every opportunity he gets. It's a slippery slope. One minute it's fun, and the next you've gone too far and can't claw your way back. I can see why it drives his brother and sister mad that he's his mother's favorite.

Love is blind to many things, and Terri's obsession with her son allows him the freedom to get away with literally anything. It's not my place or my business, but I know myself. I'm going to end up stepping in, and when I do, it's going to be on some people's toes.

It's decided that everybody is getting ready and heading off in a couple of hours. Everyone except me, with strict instructions to go to bed and stay there, and Pacey, who's staying behind with Gus. The assistants and Chef have the day off, too, so they're heading into town.

I am chomping at the bit to be alone with him again.

One by one, they all head back to their rooms, but he hangs back. "Want to come down to the beach?"

"I got very little sleep last night —"

"Why?" His face is a picture of concern. "What were you doing?"

*You have to be kidding me, right?* "Girls' night turned into all-night chat with your sister, mostly involving her talking about how amazing Jean-François is. You didn't hear us?" He breaks into the most relieved grin. "What did you think I was doing? Or rather who?"

"No. I didn't... I'm sorry."

Yesterday his hands were everywhere. I was this close to sleeping with him, and today he's convinced I spent the night with his brother...or maybe Jean-François, perhaps? Clearly I'm the slut of the villa.

"Pace..." *God damn it.* "You *have* to trust me."

He comes right up close to me, closer than he's ever been in public before. This is wild. It's like he no longer gives a shit about being found out. "I do trust you, Tuppence Farthing. It's hard, you know, to accept that you really want *me*."

"Oh, I want you," I reply, moistening my lips just at the idea of how much I want his mouth on mine. He flexes his hands, rubs them on the sides of his jeans. Anything to not touch me right, here, right now.

Gus gives a jealous bark, bringing us right out of any dirty thoughts we might have been having. He jumps up at Pace's leg, wanting to be picked up.

"I'll meet you in the kitchen at around twelve. We'll make lunch together."

"Sure," he replies, picking up our furry child. "It's a date, isn't it, Gus? Now let's go for the longest walk on the beach. We're going to play all morning then this afternoon everybody gets a long nap."

Naptime. I'm counting down the hours.

# Chapter Eighteen

*Pace*

Gus attacks the very evil seaweed.

"Good job, little guy."

I sometimes wonder how I ended up owning a dog and what the fuck I'm going to do with him when I get back to my little apartment, but I think it's clear to both of us that we're family now.

I do my best to sound sincere, but all I want to do is sleep. My eyes are literally closing over. He looks up at me with his little tongue hanging out, and I forget the exhaustion. I'll stay up every night for this little guy.

"Hey," says Penny, walking down toward us. Her dress wafts around in the sea breeze. She lifts her head, breathes in the sea air and exposes that long slim neck of hers. My breath hitches and I throw my hand to my chest.

*Fuck*, I'm in deep.

"Hey. I thought you were spending the morning in your room."

She grins. "It's twelve-thirty."

"It is?" I guess time got away from us.

She sits down beside me on the beach towel, a hamper in hand. "I brought lunch—and treats for the baby."

"You thought of everything."

"Well, Chef made the food, but I grew up in a home that had almost as many pets as there were children. I'm British, and we do pets like no other. I couldn't bring something for us and nothing for this little guy." Gus tilts his little head as if he's in total agreement and gets a cuddle for his troubles. "Could I now, huh? You're a good boy. Yes, you are."

"I grew up in a household where staff did everything for us, including changing my sister's diapers. I'll take any advice you can give me on how to handle a puppy. It won't be long before this guy is twice this size and eating everything I own."

I pull Gus onto my lap, and she hands me the towels.

"Is he all better now?"

"I think I understood with my very poor Spanish that he probably ate something he shouldn't have. The vet gave him something which made him…uh…poop—which he did, a lot, everywhere—and now we just wait and see."

"I can watch him for you when we've finished, if you like. You can go get showered, shaved, all that."

I ruffle my hair. I must look terrible. This is not how I planned to start things with Penny. I've spent the last week doing my hair and flexing my muscles, but today, I'm rocking the Dan look, which involves greasy hair and smelling like yesterday. "Do I look that bad?"

"No, of course not." She winks at me. "Thought you might need a break, that's all."

She lets out this little giggle and my stomach flips over. *Fuck*, I'm in deep with Penny. She's constantly on my mind. That smile. *That* body. She's right about me needing to trust her, but I'm terrified that Dan is going to waltz in and steal her from under my nose. I can't even go there. Like, it literally hurts to think about it.

"I...uh." Damn it, brain. Say something. "Thank you." I fight the urge to kiss her for the second time today — not because somebody might see us, but because she's right. I'm looking rough. I need to freshen up before I pull this gorgeous woman into my arms and finish what I started last night.

We eat. Finger food, fruit, chips — the perfect summer beach picnic. Gus jumps around us, kicking up the sand and nibbling on his expensive treats.

I go to get up, and he whimpers and runs over to me. "Stay with Penny. I'll be right back."

I stop at the bottom of the steps and turn to look back. How is it possible to know a person for only a few days and feel like this about them? Not just the butterflies and the hormones. A deeper connection. The kind that makes you never want it to end.

Fuck. I'm turning into bridezilla. That 'forever' stuff is dangerously viral. I've caught *all* the feels.

* * * *

*Penny*

Pace steps out of the shower, a towel around his waist, looking like a fucking dream, and I try to breathe. I have Gus in my arms. This is not the time to get all giddy. He catches me checking him out and leans into the doorway.

"Can I help you?"

"You sure can. Someone was getting a little tired, so we packed up and came in. Plus, it's getting really dark out there. Did they predict storms today?"

"I don't know. I've hardly looked at my phone in days."

"Me neither." It's super weird for me to not check my phone. Half of my business involves managing my gigs, posting my music online and keeping in touch with fans. I promised myself that a holiday was a holiday and put everything on hiatus. Even my PA took a couple of weeks off. I was pretty mad with the world before I came away, and I didn't want to be reminded of any of it by going online.

He pops his head out of the French doors. "Whoa, you're not kidding. It looks pretty bad out there." The clouds are getting darker by the minute.

"Here," I say, handing him the puppy. "You get him cleaned up and I'll do a tour of the property and shut all the windows."

I rush around the house, closing it up as best I can, then I tiptoe back to Pace's room.

"Is he asleep?"

"Out like a light." He closes the door to the balcony. "Shall we, uh… Do you want to go to your room?"

He's all nervous and cute. "Sure."

He stands in my doorway, his hands on his hips, not allowing me to get past. "Wow, your room is neat."

It is. I changed my bedsheets after my late-night party. Plus, I tidied, just in case.

I squeeze past him, wrapping my hands around his waist as I go and sliding my hand across the front of his trousers. As if there was any doubt about what we're going to do right here, right now, I'm staking my claim.

"It's an illusion. I'm not known for my tidiness."

He grins. "Thank God, me neither." That's something that someone who wants to date you would say. Someone who sees a future.

That's not what I'm looking for. *Am I?*

He'll leave me broken-hearted. This handsome guy who lives halfway around the world from me is definitely destined to break my heart.

We stand there awkwardly, each waiting for the other to make a move. He sits on the bed and I step forward between his legs.

I climb onto him, one leg then another. Face to face, eyes locked, I place my mouth on his and eat up his gasp as I rub down onto his crotch. I want him. I want to fuck this man. His cock, hard and ready, is bursting out of his shorts.

He wraps his arms around me as we fall back onto the bed, sliding his hand under my T-shirt and skimming my skin. His touch is so gentle, so deliberate. The longing to feel those fingers on my pussy turns me on so much. I need this man inside me.

I sit back up, looking down over his prostrate body, rip off my T-shirt, revealing my bikini, then pull on the strings, showing him my breasts for the first time. His gaze doesn't falter. He is savoring every second.

He sits up, circles his tongue around the very tip of my nipple. My pussy clenches. I don't want to mess around, take my time. I want him *now*.

I pull my breast from his mouth. "Fuck me."

"Isn't that what I'm doing?"

I crumble to the bed next to him, tug at my shorts, pulling my thong off as I go, exposing myself completely to him. "No, I don't want to wait. I want you to fuck me *now*."

He chuckles. "Okay, wow, I thought women liked to take their time."

"Not today."

He stands up, pulls his shorts down and climbs over me, hovering his cock over my pussy. He grabs a condom from the bedside table. When did he put that there?

Pace seems like a guy who always comes prepared...literally.

I take it from him, open it and roll the condom onto his cock. That little choking sound he makes when he's turned on makes me squirm with excitement. It's so *fucking* hot.

I want to know what he sounds like when he makes love. I want him to gasp and moan and scrunch his face up as he comes.

He lowers his body down the bed.

"No," I say almost too abruptly. "I can't wait."

"Uh-uh," he replies, shaking his head. "If we're doing this, we're doing this right. I want to taste you." He lunges at my pussy with his mouth, making me squirm with pleasure.

*Holy fuck.* I really want him, but *God*, that is good. I guess if it makes him happy...

I can't help but think about how much I hated this when I was with Reece, how much I resented him going down on me, because it was so very, very bad.

But this isn't Reece, and this isn't bad. This is something else entirely. He slides his tongue down from my clit and licks at my pussy, then I feel the slick tightness of his fingers as they enter me.

Still fucking me with his hand, he moves back up the bed and stares me in the eyes. "I want to see your face when you come."

I bite my lip, hard, as he brushes his thumb across my clit.

"Good?"

"Mm-hmm."

He's so dominant, so in control. A whole new Pacey. The things this man can do when he liberates himself from his battered-down shell…

"You want more." He flicks his thumb back and forth against my clit as he moves his fingers slowly in and out of me. "Moan for me."

I gasp and groan as the excitement builds then grab onto his hand, pushing it farther inside me, holding him to me as the waves of my orgasm rock my body. I cry out his name and stare into that delicious face of his as he brings me to climax.

We lie there, transfixed, as I find my breath, his beautiful green eyes boring into my soul. His breath is as rapid as mine. His gaze never leaving my eyes for a second, he takes away his hand, rolls on top of me and enters me. We fit perfectly within one another, our two bodies entwined, my arms and legs wrapped around him, holding him as tight as I possibly can.

He nudges my face with his, kisses my lips, closes his eyes and fucks me slowly, barely moving his body as the gentle rhythm of his cock grows faster and he seems to get even harder.

His face contorts as the moment gets away from him. He tries to slow down, tries to move his hand between us, but I pull him to me, the intense desire to see him come, to bring him to fruition excites me. I don't want him to stop.

The two of us are totally in sync as he judders and empties himself, barely allowing a second orgasm to rise within me. I want him to feel me, to fuck me. I want him to come inside me. I hold him to me, grasping onto his back with the very tips of my fingers as he releases the frustration that has been building inside him since the previous night, maybe even since we met.

His eyes widen. He hilts his breath. "Crap, fuck, I'm sorry. That was so quick. I'm totally good at this, I swear."

Now I feel bad for not letting him do his thing. He looks so ashamed, embarrassed by his performance.

I chuckle and kiss him on the nose. "It's my fault. I didn't want you to stop."

He laughs nervously. "It's been a while."

"It was amazing. You know that, right? You're amazing."

"Wow, you're easily pleased. You wait until I'm ready again, because if you think that was good, what's coming next will blow your fucking mind."

# Chapter Nineteen

*Penny*

"Hey, honey, are you feeling better?"

I open my eyes to see Terri's face leering at me through the curtain.

*Fuck this big glass house with its fucking French doors and fucking huge balconies.*

Pace's arm is strewn across me, his gentle snores tickling my ear. I nudge him and he looks up at me, all dopey. He flashes me a satisfied, loving grin and pecks me on the nose.

"I love you," I whisper. I have to tell him before the shit hits the fan. I can't let him go without him knowing how I feel. But this is bad and it's going to get so much worse for both of us.

His eyes widen. "Wha — ?"

"I love you," I whisper through gritted teeth.

"Love you, too," he replies, going in for the smooch and stopping short as he sees the horror in my eyes.

"Pacey James Scott!"

"*Fuck.*" He groans, not even bothering to move or look up at his own mother.

My mind whirs with all the different things I could say to make it not look like I just slept with my fiancé's brother.

*Fuck indeed.*

"No," says his mom, pushing away someone else on the balcony. "You don't want to see this."

"Oh, I do," replies Emma gleefully. As much as she has become my friend, she clearly wants to be in on the drama that is about to unfold.

The door swings open and all eyes swivel toward Dan, who is creeping in. "Pen, the weather took a turn for the worse and —"

"Dan!" I cry, trying to think of something, anything to say.

He stops in his tracks, takes a second to evaluate the situation, then throws his hands to his face in shock, in the worst example of acting I have ever seen.

*Oh, Dan, really?*

I am never watching any of his movies ever again. I was bamboozled by his looks into thinking that he had talent. "What the *fuck*?" he screams.

"It's not... I'm sorry." I search desperately for the words that will make this right, play along with the overly theatrical dramatics. I'm still contractually obliged to comply with this charade.

"How could you do this to me?" Dan falls to his knees. He's actually crying real tears now, big ugly scbs as his face falls to the floor. *Oh my God*, this is so embarrassing. "My own brother."

Is he talking to me or Pace? The sound of Gus barking comes from next door. Pace, who has not said a word or reacted in any way up until now, emits a deep sigh and goes to get up. He looks under the sheet then at everyone in the room. "I'm going to need someone to pass me my shorts." The atmosphere is electric. Kelli and Karl have appeared at the door, and I can even see Pace's dad peeping over his wife's shoulder. *Yay.* The whole family's here. Nobody moves. "Please. I need to sort out the dog."

Dan comes out of his sobbing state and grabs his brother's shorts, throwing them in his direction. "Here."

Pacey slips them on under the sheets and gets up to go deal with Gus. "Oh, get over it." He steps over Dan's prostrate body. "You never loved her, and you hardly know her. If you did, you'd have never let her go. She's the most fantastic woman I've ever met. If you really wanted her, you'd never have let me steal her away." Impressive acting, if a little harsh.

"Pacey!" his mother shouts after him as he leaves the room. "Pacey, come back here!"

"Mom, please," says Dan. "I'd like to speak to Penny alone." She acquiesces and shushes everybody away.

He sits up on the bed next to me, the two of us face to face. Now that everyone is gone and the show is over, his crocodile tears dry up completely and his frown turns into an uncomfortable grimace.

"I'm sorry, Dan."

He shakes his head. "One week, one fucking week, and all you had to do was keep your pants on around my brother."

I pull the sheet up to cover myself. "I have no excuse. I'm sorry. Maybe this is a good thing."

Dan looks at me as if I've lost it. "What? Why?"

"All this was to convince your parents to leave your love life alone."

He squints at me. "And?"

"And now that you're all broken-hearted, they're going to expect you not to settle down and get a girlfriend for a while. This is perfect, and you come out of it smelling like roses." Unlike Pace, who gets to be the bad guy once again. From the sound of the raised voices in the room next door, the blame game has already begun.

"We did have to break up at some point. It's sad. I was getting used to having you around."

I throw him my best dismissive look. "You've hardly spent a moment with me since we got here."

"But every moment I spent with you was so... special." He puts his hand on my cheek. "I loved seeing you again, and I really liked the idea of being normal — of people thinking I was normal, at least."

Oh, my sweet Dan, who carries the weight of the world on his shoulders and hides it so spectacularly well.

"There's nothing wrong with the way you live your life, Dan. You *are* normal. Well..."

"Well what? I'm going to get relationship advice from the brother-fucker?

"Oh you're funny. *Hilarious.* No, you need to be more honest with the men and women who end up in your bed. For someone who's supposedly good at reading people, you sure don't notice when someone has fallen in love with you."

"Kelli?" I nod. "I told her I don't get involved. I warned her not to get too attached. That's not on me."

"But you didn't walk away when she did. In fact, you took her back for more."

He drops his hand to his lap and looks down then plays with the sheet, winding the corner around his finger. "I…I like having someone who loves me. The whole fake lovey-dovey thing we had going on felt so good. I like hearing her tell me that she loves me."

Sometimes I want to throttle him.

*Let yourself be loved.*

"Then why break her heart? She's open and willing to do what you want to do, and you need to respect that. There aren't a lot of women out there who are into sharing their man."

Kelli is a much braver woman than I will ever be.

"I'll get hurt," he replies, his voice cracking. It's been five years, and he still isn't over it.

My heart breaks for Dan. All this time and he still hasn't found his way. Everybody can see it, but nobody does anything to help. His parents pretend that everything is fine and his siblings hate him for it. "Dan, you have to move on. You have to believe that you *can* be loved. Maybe what you're doing and how you're doing it needs to be tweaked a little to bring you more joy. Promise me you'll talk to someone – *without* luring them into your bed."

He throws me a sly grin. "I talk to you, and I never lured you into my bed."

"Only because you know I'd say no."

He runs his hands down his chest and swivels his hips. "Never. You know you want all of this." I push him away and he falls back onto the bed beside me. "You're the best, Penny. You always were. Pace is a lucky guy."

"Not at the moment, he's not. He's getting a rollicking from your parents. I can take the fall for this, all the blame, but you have to forgive him...publicly. You owe me that, at least."

"A 'rollicking'? Where do you find these words? Is it an unsavory rollicking?"

"Shut up and go save your brother."

We spend a couple of minutes formulating a plan. Dan is completely opposed to my idea, but I don't give him the choice. I have the least to lose here. God only knows why, but these boys insist on staying in their parents' good books, despite their mother's behavior. This is the only way it can go, with me being the villain of the story.

While I shower and pack my bag, Dan is next door pulling his brother into his arms. He is explaining my devilish plan to his concerned family. I can even hear Emma giving shocked 'oohs' and 'aahs' for effect.

Worried that Dan wasn't paying me enough attention, I seduced Pace, taking advantage of him and his attraction for me. I convinced him to sleep with me, and in a moment of weakness, he fell for my seductive charms. Dan has come to realize what a terrible person I am and doesn't hold his brother responsible for any of it. In fact, he's glad this happened so that he found out exactly what kind of person I really am.

As their voices carry through the open window, I can hear Pace insisting that this is all made-up and his family telling him that he's wrong and that it has to be all my fault. Everybody fell for my dreadful, conniving lies.

*Play the game, damn it, Pace. You want so desperately to be loved by your parents. Don't let this destroy any hope of them forgiving you. Don't be an idiot, Pacey Scott.*

I'm kind of hurt that they fell for this so easily. I let out a little derisive chuckle as I close up my suitcase.

Was I that unlikeable to my future in-laws? Dan and Pace's parents really are the worst.

The sound of arguing dissipates. My bags are packed and ready to go. Dan offered to organize somewhere for me to stay for the next few days until I can get a flight. I sneak into Kelli's room where she's hiding out and tell her that I'd insisted Dan let her stay on here as long as she wants. They need to have a long talk, and they can do that now with me out of the way. I suggested she make herself scarce in case Terri gets it into her head to try to convince her son to throw her out, too.

I'm in no rush to get back to an empty house. Karl has made it known where I am and who I'm with on every one of Dan's social media accounts. Public interest in me and the men I'm dating has not yet died down.

No rush to go home at all.

I just need to be far enough away from these people to resist the desire to come back and fight for Pace.

I promised myself that I wouldn't get involved.

I promised myself that it was just the one time.

I open the door, blocking it with my foot as I grab all my bags. He stands there, red-eyed, barring my way.

"Stay," he croaks, his voice rough from crying. "I need you to stay."

# Chapter Twenty

*Pace*

She shakes her head and tries to push past me, but I stand my ground. She can't go. I won't allow it. This has to stop here — all the lies, the control. My family have hurt enough people. I can't let them hurt her, too.

"Please."

She shakes her head. "I can't."

"You can. I'll explain everything. It's all Dan's fault, anyway. He took advantage of your broken heart and you being publicly humiliated." I'm still mad with him about that, but that discussion can wait.

"What?"

*Crap.* I'm so bad at getting all the words out in the correct order, and I have to get this right. She *has* to stay. "No... I didn't mean... Not publicly humiliated. He told the entire Internet that you were together and... Look... I'm not the bad guy here, remember? Stay."

"I can't. I promised Kelli. I promised her that I wouldn't do this — no relationships, no boyfriend, no babies, no marriage."

Damn Kelli and her constant interfering. I get that she wants the best for Penny, but that's me. Nobody will ever love Penny as much as I do right now.

"Kelli doesn't decide your life for you. She's fucking Dan." I lower my voice, aware that I'm throwing everybody under the bus. "I'm not proposing, and I wasn't suggesting that we buy a little house and pop out a few babies. I just want to get to know you better."

"We had sex. It was nice." She sighs, smiles at me and taps her hand against my chest.

"Three times, to be precise, and the last two were pretty incredible, if I do say so myself. It was good, wasn't it? We were good."

She doesn't flinch. Her mouth is fixed into a permanent frown, but her eyes tell a different story. "It was *very* nice. You were *very, very* good at it. You were..." She grips tightly onto my chest, and I know she's doing this for Dan and me — and because of her stupid promise to Kelli. I know she wants to stay.

"Great. Yeah, I get it. So it was just a fling, just you scratching an itch?"

She cracks. Tears form in her perfect, beautiful eyes. "*No*. Well, yes. No! You don't get it. Look at you, being all handsome and gorgeous and perfect boyfriend material and I will fall in love with you and I will want to marry you and I will want to have cute babies with you and that will scare you and you will run away."

I put my hand over hers, holding it to my chest. Can't she feel how much my heart belongs to her? I want that with her, all of it, the real deal. Can't she see? "I'm not Rick, and you're the one running away."

"Reece."

*For fuck's sake.* "Reece… I'm not him. I'm not any of them. I'm not going to get scared and run away. I'm not saying that I'm going to marry you, either. In case you haven't noticed, Penny, I'm a nice guy."

*I'm the fucking best thing that could ever happen to you. Stay with me.*

"I can't." She rips her hand from mine.

"Penny, please."

She shakes her head and her face crumples. Penny's trying so hard to please everyone but herself. "I promised. I can't. Don't follow me. Don't tell our secrets, any of them. Protect your brother. Promise me." Protect Dan? She has to be kidding me. *Oh my God,* it's always Dan. She grabs my chin and pulls my face down to hers. "Be the brother he needs, and he might surprise you."

She tries to push past me, but I can't let her go. I can't face never seeing her again. I can't lose her.

Dan puts a hand on my shoulder. "Let her go, man."

"How can you say that? How can you do this, let her take all of the blame, after everything she did for you? I thought you loved her."

"Pacey." My mom steps in, pushing Dan out of the way and grabbing at my arm. "She's not worth it."

I glare at Dan, begging him to do the right thing. *What the fuck, man?* I don't want to tell anybody what Penny told me, but damn it, he's going to let that sweet girl get kicked out of this house, after all she's done for him.

I raise a fist to my own brother. "How could you? It's *Penny.* She—"

"Pacey, don't you dare." She stares at me, her face turning bright red, her eyes boring into my soul. She drops her bags and points a finger at my chest. "Don't. You. Dare. This is my fault. End of story."

Dan looks at the two of us. He opens his mouth to speak, finally getting some kind of a conscience. "Pen—"

"*Oh my God*. Now is not the time to be noble, Dan. Drop it. I'm leaving and that's it. Now let me through, please."

She pushes past me and heads down the stairs. I go to follow her but Dan wraps his arms around me, holding me there. "She's going to leave, Dan," I utter, defeated.

"Let her go, dude. Let her go."

She was literally just in my arms telling me she loves me, and now, she's going. "I can't."

She doesn't stop. She just keeps on walking right out of the house, right out of my life. I look at Dan. I look at my parents. Someone's going to stop her. Someone's going to tell them. Someone has to do something.

"Good riddance. I never liked her anyway," says Mom with a sneer.

"What?" says Dan. He swings around and looks at her, then at me. There's no doubt in either of our minds who the real villain of our story is. The woman who left Dan on the brink of killing himself at only sixteen years old and the same person who's been blaming me for everybody else's problems my whole life. "Shut the fuck up!" he yells, his face turning to thunder.

She lifts a finger, points at us both. "Don't you—"

"Terri, enough!" says my dad, grabbing her by the arm and dragging her back to her room. She says nothing. In my life I've seen my father raise his voice two, maybe three times. She knows when he means business, and right now, he is mad as hell.

*Fuck.*

*Everything's fucked.*

Emma comes out of her room with Gus in her arms. "I think he's hungry or something, I don't know."

"Thank you. I'll take him."

She looks down at her feet. "I'm sorry I didn't help. I didn't know what to do."

"It's okay. It's mine and Dan's mess. There wasn't really anything you could have done."

She smiles at me, a conciliatory smile from an enemy who has become a friend. "For what it's worth, I thought she was pretty amazing."

"She is," says Dan, "and I'm sorry, too." He pats me on the back. "I fucked up, like I always do, and everybody else gets to suffer."

Penny's words echo in my mind. Dan's not the big, strong, independent guy I always thought. He needs me and Em. He needs his family.

Penny is gone, and I couldn't stop her. She made her choice — the wrong one — and I have to accept it.

"I'm going to my room," I say.

"No," says Dan, putting a hand on my shoulder. "You don't want to be alone tonight." He tells Em to get Kelli and suggests that we go downstairs and play cards and watch old movies and drink too many shots.

"Sounds cool," says Em. "There's a hell of a storm brewing."

I look outside. Dan wouldn't have let Penny go without some kind of arrangement, but I don't like to think of her alone tonight...or ever. She should be with me.

"She'll be fine," he says, looking at my worried face. "Karl called a car and booked the best hotel. I'll call her later."

Dan and Emma head downstairs, already arguing about which movie they're going to start with. I grab Gus and some of his chew toys. He gets to come play happy families, too.

I don't want to be with them. I want to chase after Penny. I want to make things right. I want my heart to stop feeling like someone has punched it so hard that it cracked into a million pieces.

I tiptoe past my parents' room. My dad is berating my mom. It's like I've jumped into another dimension where my brother is not actually a bad person, my sister is not a complete bitch whenever I try to talk to her and my dad has finally woken up to my mom's behavior.

I walk down the stairs and resist the temptation to just keep on walking. I have siblings I need to get to know.

Penny left of her own free will. She chose not to stay with me, and I have to face that fact. It's time to mend some fences.

# Chapter Twenty-One

*Penny*

Why does *every* modern building on this island have to be made from ninety-eight percent glass? The hotel is a fine example of this, with marble floors, glass elevators and windows as far as the eye can see.

I check in and the porter takes me through the building past the restaurant and bar and out to the beautiful pools. We hop in a golf cart and he drives me to my apartment.

I didn't grow up with money. In fact, the early years of my life were extremely poor, compared to modern standards. When I made a huge amount of money at the very ripe age of sixteen, I had absolutely no idea what to do with it. I knew that I didn't want to spend it or live like a queen. On the advice of my very expensive financial consultant, I invested it and created a foundation for foster kids. Nobody should have to leave home and, afterward, have to fend for themselves. I give them a helping hand to buy a flat, get a job or go to university.

So when I do get to feel like a princess — which I'm doing today because I'm thoroughly fucked off with the world — I do it in style. Go big or go home. And I don't really have a home to go back to.

The apartment has a sea view and every luxury item I could ever need or wish for. Karl thought of everything, all at Dan's expense. Why the fuck not? He owes me for that debacle. Well, okay, the whole 'falling in love with his brother' thing is totally my bad, but other than that, he owes me for stepping in and at least trying to look like I was his girlfriend.

What to do first? Take a dip in my private Jacuzzi or just empty the wine collection — or do both. Anything to stop me thinking about Pace.

No more late-night card playing, fending off mosquitoes and downing cocktails. No more mornings stretched out on the balcony or walking Gus on the beach.

No more kisses that leave a little stubble burn or touches that thrill me. No more making sweet, sweet love with that beautiful man. Pace is out of my life forever. I made damn sure of that.

The porter pockets his tip and leaves. The quiet is deafening so I pick up my phone to call Kelli.

"Hey, sweetie, you doing okay?" she says, her voice filled with worry. I can hear people talking in the background. "Hold on. I'm just going to take this outside." She tells someone that it's her mum on the phone, and the voices fade.

"Hey…" I hardly get the word out before the tears flood from my eyes. I tell her everything that was said, in between the heavy sobs of regret.

"Oh, Penny… If it's any consolation, there's a bunch of broken-hearted men here, too."

I throw myself on the bed. "That doesn't really help. Should I come back? Have I made a terrible mistake?"

"*No*. Terri and Bob had a huge row. She's decided to turn over a new leaf and be a better mother to her kids. What a joke. First thing she did was announce that you are *persona non grata* and that we're never to mention you again. You can imagine how well that went down. Dan and Pacey shouted at her, then she stormed back off up to her room. She was that close to chucking me out, too, but everybody insisted I stay."

I fiddle with my hair. Has he mentioned me? Did he run after me? I bite hard into my lip. No. I did this for him, so she wouldn't be so hard on him. "Has she forgiven Pacey?"

"Honey, I don't know. I don't think so."

"Ugh. I signed a contract. I made a legal promise and got paid for it. I sold away my right to sleep with whoever I wanted for one whole week. I should have just kept my knickers on." I made my bed and now I have to lie in it…*alone*.

"Do you want me to come to the hotel? Are you going to be okay?"

I peer out of the window. The dark clouds that sent everybody scurrying back to shore this afternoon are now looking even more ominous. "No. I'm going to go for a bit of an explore, then probably hunker down for the night. That storm looks scary. I'll be fine."

I chat for a little longer then she has to go. As I cut the call, I notice at least three messages from Dan. I switch off the phone and throw it onto the bed. No need for more hassle tonight. He had every chance to come clean, but he didn't. I broke his trust, I know, but if his mother was going to forgive anybody for lying, it would have been him.

That woman has convinced every one of her children that they can't live or breathe without her love and acceptance, and while I hate her for it, I can't stand between them and their mother. Family is a privilege denied to many, and I'm not going to interfere in theirs.

After changing into something prettier than the mismatched clothes I'd thrown on when I'd packed my bags, I stroll back up to the hotel. The pools are deserted, the wind is rising and the palm trees surrounding the hotel are starting to sway.

I dive into the bar. The large metal clock on the wall reminds me that it's only three o'clock, but the number of people milling around, glasses in hand, is reassuring. My desire for a tequila shot or two is not going to look too ridiculous at this time of the day.

A very handsome older barman comes over as I perch on a stool. "What can I do you for?"

"Ooh, you're English, nice to meet a fellow compatriot. I'll have a tequila shot, please, and you might as well line up a second and a third."

He smiles, kindly. "Someone break your heart?"

"You're good at this — well, almost — I think I broke his."

He puts the tiny glass down in front of me and fills it. "Did you now? Going around breaking hearts like that, I'll have to watch out."

"Ah, you're out of luck. After the last couple of weeks, I'm never dating again. *Get thee to a nunnery.*"

He places an elbow on the bar and leans his head on it. "That bad, huh? Want to talk about it?"

I shake my head and down my shot.

He serves me a second then a third and my tongue loosens. "...so, she's right and I know she's right, because she knows everything about relationships and love and I just go from one disaster to another. And it's never going to work because he lives on the other side of the world and he's going to be a doctor, even though he loves me."

He frowns. "He loves you? Did he tell you he loves you?"

"Yes."

He offers me a fourth, but I turn the glass upside down. My head is spinning. "Look... Perhaps I'm stepping in where I don't belong here, but can I give you some advice?"

"Sure."

He smiles. "There are no rules."

"That is very strange advice."

He hesitates, then rubs his hands together. "I don't know where you got the idea in your head that there are a set of stages in a relationship or that people in love *have* to live happily ever after or that you have to have kids or whatever, but you're wrong. There are *no* rules."

"You keep saying that."

He shrugs. "Marry or don't. Live together for a year then split up. Have two boyfriends, or three — or maybe a whole bunch of boyfriends and girlfriends."

"Sounds like someone I know."

His eyes widen. "Do I want their number?"

I chuckle. "Oh yeah, you want his number. Anyway, serve me another drink, something non-alcoholic, and tell me some more about this rules thing."

"Your doctor guy. He loves you and you love him, right?" I nod. "And he wants to be with you, even though it might cause friction with his parents, but his parents don't like much about him, anyway."

"Uh-huh."

He pours me a Coke from a glass bottle, sticking a slice of lemon in it, before pushing it toward me. "And you want to be with him, but you think that means he's got to get married and have babies with you."

"Well, when you put it like that…no, he doesn't *have* to."

"Nobody *has* to do anything. When it comes to relationships, it's about the boundaries that you set between you and your partner. That's it. If you want to see how it goes, tell him that. If he thinks marriage might be in the cards one day but not for another year or even ten years, then you need to decide if that's what *you* want. If you want to be with him for now, then be with him and just let tomorrow decide for you. How about that?"

That is so wise. So sensible. Why don't people tell you these things when you start dating? Why does it all have to be so formulated? Adulting is hard enough, but it's even harder when you haven't got a clue what you're doing.

"It might be the tequila, but you really sound like you're making sense."

He winks at me. "Trust me. I haven't had a drop, and I'm making a lot of sense."

He really was. I need to talk to Pacey. I need to tell him how I really feel and about the rules — or the lack of them. I should take the barman with me. That would be an excellent plan. He can just explain the whole thing then I'll introduce him to Dan and Kelli. She always did like an older man.

*Fuck.*

Pacey's really far away…and I'm a little bit tipsy.

"Thank you. I think I know what I need to do. But first I need a nap."

"You do, and you need a ride down to your apartment. Hold on. I'll get someone to cover me and we'll take a buggy. So tell me more about this guy whose number I have to have."

"Well," I reply with a chuckle as he gently ushers me out of the bar, "that's a funny story."

# Chapter Twenty-Two

*Pace*

"Uh, guys." Karl stands in front of the TV, just as Darth Vader is about to reveal his true identity.

"This better be important, Karl," says Dan, leaning sideways to look around his PA.

"We just received a call from the local mayor's office. There's a heavy tropical storm headed our way in a few hours and they are evacuating all of the seafront houses. They are advising us to go to the other side of the island."

Gus jumps up onto my lap and I hold him, reassuring us both. "Tropical storm? Like how bad is this tropical storm? Guys, if they think we should leave, we should leave, right?"

As if to confirm any doubts that any of us might have had, the electricity cuts out.

"We're out of here," says Emma, standing up. "Karl, you order a car, no, two, and find us somewhere to go, and I'll get Mom and Dad. Dan, you round up your entourage. Pace, you need to get Gus' stuff. We'll meet back here in ten minutes." We all just stare at her. Emma's never exactly been one to take control. She claps her hands. "Come on, guys. Let's go."

Ten minutes later and we've all shoved as much as we can into a bag and we're heading out of the house.

Dan is on the phone to a hotel. "I got us a couple of apartments at the same place we booked Penny. It's completely on the other side of the island and farther inland. We should be fine." He huddles us all into a car. Taking Kelli's hand, he helps her get in and hands her her bag. I've only ever seen him be sweet like that once before. The way he is with her, reassuring her, is he in love? Romantic gestures don't come easy to Dan. I'm seeing him in a whole new light.

\* \* \* \*

The hotel is gorgeous, but the fact that it's made out of glass isn't entirely reassuring. The little cart trundles along a thin, cobbled lane, battling against the heavy winds.

"I stayed here the first time I came. The apartments are kind of dug into the hill, so they're not part of the actual hotel. We'll be fine." He ruffles Gus' little furry head. "We'll all be fine."

Leaves and other plant life whoosh past us, and I hug my puppy even tighter.

Mom and Dad are in the other cart. Mom is still not talking to any of us because we absolutely refuse to hate Penny. She's going to be *thrilled* to find out that Penny is here.

We pile out, grabbing our stuff, and run inside before we get blown away.

Dan puts down his bags then takes Gus from my arms. "Go find her, and make sure she's okay. I'll look after this little guy."

"But —"

"I've got this. Go get her."

I run out of that building as fast as my legs can carry me. According to the little map they gave us at reception, Penny's apartment is within walking distance, but I need to see her sooner. I need to know that she's safe, that she's okay. I need to hold her in my arms.

If I'm being honest, this has very little to do with hurricanes and everything to do with the fact that I love this woman.

The wind is crazy, swirling up the leaves into mini tornadoes. It is loud and scary and I don't want to be outside for long.

I tap hard on the door. "Penny."

The door opens and a woman stands there. "*Hola.*"

*Oh.* I wasn't expecting it to be anybody else. I almost swept this very nice middle-aged woman up into my arms. I look over her shoulder. "Penny Farthing?"

"Oh, *se fue, tomó sus maletas y se fue a ver a un hombre...*"

I stare at her. *Crap.* My Spanish is limited to a few basic sentences and the *Macarena.* "Hmm?"

"She gone. She gone look for man."

What the hell? What man? Me? I hope it's me.

I run back to our apartment. I've never done so much cardio in my life, and my ears are ringing. "She left..." I shout as I run into the room, trying to catch my breath. The door swings wide open and the wind howls around the apartment, sending the cards they are playing flying everywhere.

"She left?" Dan grabs his phone. "Oh *fuck,* she left me a message."

"What? What does it say?"

"She's going back to the house. *Fuck.*"

"Language!" says my mother. "Well, what are you waiting for? Go get her, one of you, whichever one of you really loves this woman."

"But—"

"We will take care of Gus and Kelli. Go find her," says Dan as he leads me back to the door. He lowers his voice. "There's a…basement in the house, and there's a door in the kitchen. You'll be safe there. I'll text you the code."

"What?"

"No time to explain. Just go make sure she's safe."

I run back outside and the wind almost carries me back to the house. The front desk refuses to call me a taxi. They have rental cars, though, says the woman, but I'll have to sign a disclaimer. The paperwork takes far too long but they eventually hand over the keys and say some kind of a prayer for me.

The mayor's office wasn't kidding when they said tropical storm. It is wild out there. Trying to keep the car on the road is a challenge.

She's worth it. I should have chased after her when I had the chance. I hope it's not too late. Fuck, I need her to be okay.

I get about five minutes from the house when I spot a chewed-up scooter on the side of the road, then I see her.

Standing there, battered and bruised.

My heart stops.

*Holy fuck.* She could have died.

"Penny?" She's limping and crying and looks like she's been dragged through a bush backward. "What the hell? What are you doing out here?"

She jumps, or rather falls, into the passenger seat. "Oh my God, am I glad to see you. I thought I was going to die out there. Turns out Vespas and hurricanes don't go well together."

"You could have been killed...or worse."

"What's worse than being killed?" she replies, letting out a pained chuckle at my panicked reply. Then she grabs my chin and pulls me to her slightly swollen mouth. "Kiss me."

*What?* I'm having a moment of complete stress here and she's making jokes.

"Did you bump your head?"

"I did, but that's not why I want you to kiss me. I had this big speech prepared, but I nearly died trying to get to you and I don't want to waste another second. Kiss me, damn it."

Despite my reticence — she's clearly not feeling like herself — I do as Penny says. Her lips are dry and salty from the coastal wind. She sinks into my arms and we fumble and grab at each other in the tiny car. The wind hurls and bustles us from outside, but just for a second we're lost in each other.

Lost and found.

"We should go to the house. It's closer, and we'll be safer. Why did you come out here? You could have died. You couldn't kiss me if you were dead."

"We really need to talk about your obsession with death. It's fascinating and terrifying at the same time." I start the engine and she sinks back into her seat. "I needed to see you to tell you about the rules — or the *not* rules. The fact that there aren't any rules. I was drinking tequila with this barman and—"

*What is she going on about?* "How bad did you hit your head when you fell off the scooter?"

"Not too hard, I don't think." She runs her hand through her hair, searching for a bump. We draw up in front of the house, and I park the car as close to the front of the building as I can. "There are no rules, you see."

"Penny, you are not making sense. Let's get you inside and look at your foot...and your head."

"I'm fine. Well, I think I sprained my ankle, but my head is *fine*."

I jump out of the car and run around, help her out then carry her into the house. Dan's doors all have battery-operated code locks, so you just have to enter it then you're in. Juggling the woman I love, my phone and trying to get the numbers in the right order in a tropical storm is challenging, to say the least, but I somehow manage to do it and we're safer than we were before.

The house is plunged into darkness. The electric blinds are all closed and there's no electricity. I put Penny down and run to the bathroom to grab a first-aid kit, then I come back, sweep her back up into my arms and kiss her again—because now that I've started, I don't want to stop—then take her through to the kitchen.

"Dan says there's some kind of secret basement. I don't know why we all couldn't hide out there during the storm, but still." I punch in another code and the door opens. Getting Penny down the tight stairway is a bit of a struggle, but I manage without hurting her any further. It feels good to have her in my arms, her body next to mine. It's reassuring. My heartbeat starts to decrease for the first time in hours. "He said something about a back-up generator switch, too." I fiddle around, phone in hand, and find something next to the electric panel.

"Is that it?" she says, pointing at a small yellow switch.

"Hopefully." I close my eyes, make a wish and turn it, opening them to see that we do indeed have light. "Holy crap." Now I know why Dan didn't want us to stay here.

"It's a fucking sex dungeon, Pace," says Penny with a grin. "I'm really not in the mood, to be honest."

"Liar."

She giggles. "Okay, but I'm going to need some painkillers first, and maybe remove a few of the twigs that are stuck in my hair."

"You look beautiful."

I can't stop looking at her. I just want to hold her in my arms and never let her go. I can't believe she's here with me.

"This place is doing it for you, huh? Oh...kay."

"Well, one of those swings would certainly take the weight off your foot." I'm joking, but that's probably not a bad idea. I lift her up and carry her over.

"Do you think it's...sanitary?" she asks as I sink her into a sex swing and fall to her feet to check her ankle.

"Well, you probably don't want to shine a blue light on this place, but it'll have to do. It looks like a sprain. Can you wiggle your toes?"

"Yes, doctor. Ooh, are we playing doctors and nurses? Are you McSteamy, or McDreamy or whatever it is?"

"McNotEvenAnInternYet, but I'll play along."

"Are you going to give me a bed bath? Take my temperature with your big red thermometer? *Oh God*, I'm sorry. I'm terrible at this."

"Don't worry, ma'am. Just lie back into that swing and let me take good care of you." She does as she's told, leaning into her makeshift hospital bed as I check to see if she has any other injuries. "Where else does it hurt?"

"Fucking everywhere." She giggles and gasps as I inspect every inch of her body. She is bruised and covered in cuts, but it's mainly superficial.

I want to scream at her, tell her how mad I am that she did something so dangerous, but at the same time, I just want to be here holding her in my arms, glad that she's alive.

Love is complicated and conflicting, but I wouldn't trade it, or her, for anything.

"I am in so much pain right now. Do we really not have any painkillers?"

"There has to be a bar here somewhere," I say. "How about we have a little drink?" My family tried to get me to drown my sorrows earlier, but I didn't want to. Alcohol always makes me soppy and that was the last thing I needed when she wasn't around. Now, though? Now I can love on her all I want.

The walls of the room either have various locking mechanisms and leather straps hanging from them or they have large mysterious cupboards with elaborately painted red wooden doors.

"What's behind door number one?" shouts Penny, as I open the first storage unit I come to.

"Whips, Madam?" There are slapping devices of all shapes and sizes.

"Useful if we're under attack," says Penny as she swings to and fro.

"Noted." The second cupboard reveals a wide and wonderful array of dildos and vibrators of all colors and sizes. I hold one up by the very tips of my fingers. "What does this one do?"

Her giggles turn to full-blown laughter when she sees the look on my face. "It's a strap-on, you know for pegging or for two women."

*Gulp.* I look over at her. "Do I even want to know what pegging is?" She bites her lip, going all shy, then explains what it means.

I throw it back into the cupboard, desperately wiping the thoughts of where that one's been from my brain.

I'm going to need to triple sanitize my whole body when we get out of this room.

Door number three is the winner, revealing a large collection of different alcohols and even soft drinks, too. I grab a bottle of whiskey and two glasses. Doctor's orders.

# Chapter Twenty-Three

*Pacey*

"You're drunk." I try to hide my worried face, but she's had quite a few sips and we're going to have to go to the hospital after the storm calms down.

"I'm not. I'm tipsy. Happy. Full of the joys of spring."

Yeah, she's drunk.

I resist the temptation to roll my eyes at her and try my sensible doctor face instead. "It's July. Does it still hurt?" I try to touch her foot again, but she plucks it from my hands. She grins at me, tipping her head to one side, and tries to pull me in for a kiss instead.

I'm learning, to my dismay, that drunk Penny is also horny, cute and funny Penny, and it's killing me. Sex, when someone has fallen off a scooter in high winds and tumbled halfway down a ditch, is never advisable. Despite her giggles, she still seems to be in a lot of pain.

"It feels better, thank you. I think the ice is working—and the whiskey." She holds up the half-empty bottle. She's only had a few swigs, but that's probably enough for today.

I take my hands away and lean back into my swing contraption chair thingy. "You realize what this means. You can't run away. You're going to have to sit there and listen to me telling you how much I love you."

"You love me. You do. And I love you, too. Isn't it wonderful?" She beams, a giant smile plastered across her face.

Only a couple of more stages to go before she gets to the deep and meaningful stage of drunkenness where you question life, the universe and everything.

"I do love you. I love that you always wear what you want. You stick vintage rock T-shirts over designer bikinis, and you look beautiful in them. For some reason, you think I'm the only person in the world who thinks your boobs are gorgeous—which I don't understand, because they're perfect. You love my twin brother almost as much as I do, probably more if I'm being honest. You make me feel needed, and attractive, and clever and everything a man should feel when he's with someone special. You're perfect for me."

She nods, sagely listening to me declare my love to her.

"Boobs," she says, almost falling off her swing in a fit of giggles.

"You're wasted." I stand up and lift her out of the contraption, taking her over to one of the beds. "I know you think that being with me is all or nothing—"

"Actually, no." She holds up a finger and leans into me, still waving it in the air. "I don't. I was wrong."

"You were?"

"People think that I'm obsessed with getting married and settling down because I didn't have that—but I did. I had the best fucking family ever. I had a mum and a dad and brothers and sisters and I had a wonderful fucking childhood. That's why I want that life. But I was wrong."

I place her on the bed. "Tell me more."

"I thought that there was a natural prorgr... prorress..."

"Progression?"

"Yes, that. I thought I had to meet the guy, fall in love — which I always do — then we had to get married. Turns out you can do whatever the fuck you like. I knew you didn't *have* to marry people, and I'm smart enough to know that you don't have to stay with people for the rest of your life."

"Uh-huh."

"You can just leave tomorrow if you want to — or not. Or get married — or not. No rules." She sits up and undoes the lid of the whiskey bottle.

*Nope, that's not a good idea.*

"Maybe you should have some water." She frowns at me. "Just a couple of sips of water then the nice doctor will hand back the whiskey if needed."

"Okay." She nods reluctantly and I head back over to the bar. I don't even want to think of the parties that my brother has had here. It has to be soundproofed, because there's no way he could have entertained here without the sound coming up through the floorboards. The storm that is supposedly raging outside is making no noise at all. The house is entirely made of glass and marble. Normally you can hear a fly fart from twenty meters away.

I grab a couple of bottles of water and head back to Penny.

She looks cute, all snuggled up in the silk sheets. I didn't really want to end up sleeping in any of the beds here because of *residue* — a shiver goes down my spine — but it does look way more comfortable than any of the other contraptions in the room. And let's be honest, unless this place has had a deep clean in the last couple of days, nowhere is entirely stain free. I lie down behind her and gently snuggle up.

"Is this good? I'm not hurting you?"

"This is perfect," she replies, spooning against me. I run my fingers through her matted hair. She slowly sinks into me as she finally drifts off. At least her body can relax and heal for a few hours.

I'm right where I want to be. Well, not in a sex bed in a sex dungeon during a storm — in the arms of the woman I love. I never expected that my life would change so much over the course of a week. I've learned so much about myself, my family, my brother and I've fallen in love.

If someone had asked me how I thought this holiday would go, I would have said at the very least boring, and at the most, a week of having to put up with my incredibly dysfunctional family, which is not boring at all.

She stirs in my arms and I put my hand on her head to calm her. "Did I fall asleep?"

"Just for a second but it's okay, you can sleep. There's not much more we can do now anyway, except wait."

"I love you, Pace."

"I know."

"Will you marry me?" she asks, turning her head around and giving me the widest grin. "Nah, I'm just kidding. No rules." She yawns and starts to drift off again. "No rules."

"Oh, I am going to marry you, if you'll have me," I reply, so gently that it doesn't wake her. "You'll see. With all the pomp and circumstance that you deserve —

then I'm going to be the husband you deserve and we're going to do everything you've ever dreamed of. You'll get to be the bride, I promise, and nobody's going to ever break your heart, ever again."

# Chapter Twenty-Four

*Day Seven*
*Penny*

We awake to the sound of somebody coming downstairs. Dan tips his head to one side and smiles at the two of us. "You're so cute." Then he sees the state of me and his jaw drops. "What the hell did you do in here last night?"

"I fell off my scooter," I reply, stretching out then remembering that every single muscle in my body hurts. "Ow."

He perches on the end of the bed and hands me a coffee. "The house made it out alive. A couple of broken windows and the garden is going to need an overhaul, but the rest is intact. We should have electricity by the end of the day."

Pace rolls over, sliding a hand around my waist and kissing the back of my neck. "Is everyone upstairs?" he asks.

"You mean is Mom still pissed? No. Dad had *another* serious talk with her, like a 'get your priorities straight' talk with her. He knew, you know, about you and me and Penny and Kelli. He knew right from the start that this was a set-up, but he didn't say a word."

Pace sits up and grabs his mug from Dan. "Really? I would have loved to have seen that."

Dan shakes his head. "It wasn't pretty. They decided to stay on at the hotel. I think Mom's had enough of family for this summer."

"What about Emma?"

"She's off to France with Jean-François. Turns out his family owns some huge winery in the south of France, and he wants to spend the rest of the summer stomping grapes and lounging around the pool with her. Mom didn't even fight it, was glad to see her go."

It's so sad, but I bite my tongue. That girl is going to need some stronger maternal figures in her life. I'm pretty sure Kelli and I could do it—better than her own mother, at the very least. "Tell her she can call me anytime. I'm here for her. And I'm only a flight away if she needs me."

Dan winks at me. "You got it."

"So you guys are moving back in?" I ask. Where does that leave us?

Dan grins like a lovesick teenager. "Kelli and I are going to spend the rest of the summer here. She says her boss would be cool about that, thinks her boss might be busy, anyway."

I lie back, snuggling into Pace's warm and welcoming chest. "Her boss is wondering if she isn't going to have to either get a new stylist or end up moving to LA when her stylist runs off with a movie star."

"California would be good," Pace says. "I know someone who lives in Cali who could put you up for a while."

*Oh yeah?* "I only have another week off, then I've got three European festivals booked." Back to the LazrBoy grind. I hate being *him* and not the real me, but it pays the bills. I just want to do my own thing. "But I think I might be free after that."

Pace pulls me in for a kiss, and Dan takes that as his cue to leave. "You mean it?" he asks as he pulls away from my lips. "You really want to come to Cali with me? I don't have much. I don't even know if I can still stay in the apartment over my parents' garage. Oh, and I'm literally booked solid for the next seven years of my life."

"Yes, absolutely I do, but this is day by day, no promises, no happy-ever-afters — not yet, at least. And I'll be getting my own place."

*Oh my God. What am I doing?* This feels so right, though, more than it ever has before. The communication, the honesty. We both know exactly where we stand.

"I will wait until you're ready, but I'm pretty sure I'm going to marry you, Penny Farthing."

Okay, maybe I didn't know quite where he stood. *Play it cool, Penny.*

"Shh…" I reply, trying not to scream with joy at the fact that this guy proposed to *me*, actually wants to marry *me* and I'm saying, '*I'll think about it.*' "You'll awaken Bridezilla."

He laughs and holds me to him. "*Shit*. Nobody wants that!" I jokingly tap him on the arm. "I do have the suit, though. I did this photo shoot for Dan, years ago. He was sick and they flew me over last minute.

Top hat and tails, waistcoat and cravat, the whole shebang. Mom kept it – in case of a top-hat emergency, I guess."

*What the fuck?*

Perfect Husband Dan in the photo is actually Perfect Husband Pace? Kelli is going to *scream* when she hears this. Looks like it really was destiny after all. He was there all the time. I just had to stop looking for him.

# Epilogue

*Penny*

Gus snuggles into my lap, rubbing his little head into my stomach and getting comfortable for the drive. "How far is it to France?"

"Only three hours or so," replies Pacey, turning his head to smile at me, "then it's only a couple of hours until the hotel, so about five in all. We can make it in one go, with only a stop for this guy to pee. Should arrive just in time for lunch."

Gus has taken surprisingly well to traveling in a campervan. When he isn't on my lap, he's in his crate, munching on a treat. He's such a good little doggy. We never discovered how he came to be in Dan's life. He doesn't remember quite how he ended up owning a dog, but he's pretty sure somebody gave it to him. Whatever the circumstances, he has found his forever home with us.

The van had been Dan's idea. I have to go back up to France for my next gig, but neither of us wanted the holiday to end. Karl arranged it in minutes. We're driving up through Spain to France, then Pace is staying around for my first two gigs before heading on home. First stop, La Rochelle. My PA is going to meet us there with everything I need, including the infamous LazrBoy mask, and we'll be good to go.

This way we get to enjoy being alone together, if you don't count the little guy, before Pace has to fly home.

Home. That's a funny thing. I had no home when I came here. Everything I own had been boxed up and stored in Kelli's spare room. It looks like it might be being shipped over to California in the next few weeks if Pace has his way.

He's adamant that when he says he wants to make a real go of our relationship, he truly intends to do it — even if it does mean taking it one day at a time. The lesson has been learned. No more talk of weddings and forever. Live for today and worry about tomorrow later.

Pacey's phone beeps and I check it for him. "Did they get home okay?" His parents, while still not talking to their kids, have assured us that they will let us know when their flight landed. "Yes. Your mom has sent some kind of rambling, half-hearted apology. It's something, I guess."

He shrugs his shoulders and lets out a little sigh.

I'm not entirely sure that that woman has finished making her kids' lives a misery, but all of them are a step closer to being away from her constant negativity and judgment.

"I suppose she's trying," he replies. I place my hand on his thigh and give it a little squeeze. He wraps his fingers around mine and my heart skips a beat. This is what it's like to love and be loved without worrying if it's the right thing, where we're going or any of that.

I like to claim that my need for solidity in my relationships doesn't come from my shaky start in life, but it has to have affected the way I see the world. My foster parents gave me the home I needed, and I've been seeking that ever since, but for the first time in my life, I'm able to just breathe and enjoy what I have.

I'm not saying I'm totally cool and relaxed, either. Pace is a catch and I know that, but I'm just going to have to stay cool and work through my insecurities as they arise.

And I know that he'll be by my side as I do.

"What are you thinking about?"

"Us."

A smile creeps onto his face. "What about us?"

"Just, you know, how good it feels to be with you. I think I'm still in shock that this whole situation actually worked out for the best. Even Dan seems to be working through his shit."

Kelli texted me to say that the L word has been bandied about. Not quite in an 'I love you' kind of way, but more 'I can see myself loving you'. That's huge for Dan. Unprecedented — or, at least, not seen in a very long time. I'm so grateful that my two best friends found each other.

Of course, the idea that Kelli has grown up to possibly marry Perfect Husband Dan Scott hasn't escaped me, either. I'm just trying not to think about that too much, because it makes me *squee* with joy and upsets the dog.

"Right?" He lifts his hand from mine, pushes his glasses up his nose and runs his fingers through his mane of hair. "I really got to talk with him the other day, once the dust had settled. It's like I'm meeting him for the first time. There's so much to catch up on." He settles his hand back down onto mine. "And I have you to thank for that. We all do."

Pace's relationship with his brother is fractured from years of them being compared to each other by their mom. One conversation and a lot of hugs won't mend it, but the cracks are starting to heal. I'm so glad I'm going to be over in Cali for the next few months. I want to be part of the process, as they mend their relationship. I get to be there for my best friends *and* the man I love.

After the holidays are over, everybody gets a new start. Kelli and I will be in California working out some kind of living arrangement that allows her to see Dan without crowding him and me to see Pace without jumping into something too deep too soon. Dan is going to experience a proper relationship for the first time — open, but still being true to Kelli.

And their family is going to be just that, a family, for the first time in a long time. With or without their mother, depending on how she behaves. Even their father seems to be coming out of his shell. Standing up to his wife has made a new man of him. It's a good start, and I'm hopeful for them.

Gus lets out a little yawn, does a stretch then snuggles back into me.

The perfect life isn't what they tell you in the movies — or in books or what people expect of you. It's finding your happy place.

Right here, right now, I'm in the happiest place I can be.

"I love you," I say to Pace as a warm wave of happiness envelops me.

He smiles and squeezes my hand again. "I love you, too, Penny Farthing."

And they didn't get married, and they didn't have children, but they did live happily ever after.

# Want to see more from this author? Here's a taster for you to enjoy!

# Half Blood: Basic Witch
## Katy Hunter

### *Excerpt*

He slammed my slender wrists against the cold, hard wall, closely followed by my back. "You like it rough, huh?" I growled. "Me too."

Lifting my legs into the air, I wrapped them around his impressive waist, gripping on as tight as I could and thrusting his crotch into mine. *The guy is already hard?* This was going to be easier than I thought.

"I like it quiet." It was the first time his voice had even given a hint of who—or rather what—I was dealing with. It offered a tinge of menace, a heavy serving of control. We were definitely in demon territory.

He slammed his lips onto mine, the familiar feeling of a forked tongue snaking its way into my mouth.

He raised my wrists above my head, so he could hold them with one hand, and he started to undo his belt with the other.

I relaxed my grip around his waist and pulled my mouth away from his. This was going way faster than I'd thought. I wasn't averse to a little demon dick, but my own personal demon was quite against me sleeping with his brothers.

"Not yet." What would work? He could take me right here, right now, but I needed just a couple of more minutes. "Uh, I want to be punished. Punish me first."

His fiery red eyes lit up and I swear the cock that was pushing into my pelvis grew another five inches. "Have you been very, very bad?"

"So bad." *Like you wouldn't believe.*

Swinging me around, he flung me onto the bed and grabbed his backpack. *Lord, don't let it be teeth.* I could handle whipping, pinching, slapping—even the odd candle burn didn't break me—but oh God, I hated it when they went for the teeth.

He pulled out a leather three-tiered paddle. *Oh, bless him.* He must be new at this. I put on my most innocent face. "It won't hurt too much, will it? I know I've been naughty, but I've never done anything like this before." *Where are the boys?* If that thing hit my butt in just the right spot, I'd be coming in seconds and begging for more.

I hadn't actually planned on sleeping with this guy, but he was pushing all my buttons. It would be too hard to resist.

He rolled me over onto my stomach, brushed his hand up my thigh, grazing my stockings, and pushed up my skirt. Swirling his hand around my butt—preparing it for action—he slid his finger slowly under the gusset of my thong, brushing my clit.

"You like that?" His voice was tender, almost gentle.

*Fuck.* This big old hulking hellboy was actually a bit of a romantic. Now I knew his lineage for sure.

"Not yet… I don't want to come yet. I don't deserve it." I was really working the naughty voice tonight. A shiver of disgust went down my spine. When I was at someone's mercy, it was generally on my terms, not theirs.

Not that I was complaining... There were worse missions than getting a little action with a sex demon.

He grabbed a pair of handcuffs from his bag, the familiar clinking sending a jolt of excitement up my pussy. When did I get so hot just at the idea of a little bondage? It wasn't like my sex life was in any way boring. Quite the contrary. Maybe I was craving simpler times.

He leaned forward, attached my hands to the iron headboard and hovered over my body, the bulk of his cock rubbing against my naked butt.

The sound of hulking footsteps approached the door. I braced myself. A loud boom knocked the door straight through. The gang was finally here.

Travis grabbed hellboy by the throat and pushed him against the wall. He muttered a Latin word or two and, within seconds, the infernal fires had reclaimed their runaway.

A warm, smooth hand slid between my legs and a finger entered my pussy.

"What the hell, Cal? You're wet enough for me to take you right now," said Max, still breathless from charging into the room.

"Max, sweetheart, be a dear. Take your fingers out of me and undo these cuffs before you fuck me."

Travis muttered something about being the only one who did any work and sauntered out of the room.

The cuffs unlocked themselves and I rolled over to face my beautiful Max, my Mediterranean magic man. He fluttered those long, dark eyelashes at me and bent down to peck me on the lips.

"You took your time," I mumbled through his kiss.

"You're on a fucking yacht, Cal, in St. Tropez."

"What?" *How the hell did I get here?*

He closed his eyes and shook his head in despair. "You know how Trav gets in small boats. I had to row us here myself."

"We really need to teach that man to teleport."

He grinned, maliciously. "We need to get ourselves a decent demon."

"You're just jealous."

"Not right now, I'm not." He clasped my thighs. A few mumbled magic words and my thong was gone. "Right now, I'm about to finish what some other demon started."

# About the Author

Katy Hunter lives on a mountain in France with her husband, kids and two dogs.

When she's not writing you can find her curled up in front of the fire, book in one hand and a glass of chardonnay in the other.

Katy loves to hear from readers. You can find her contact information, website details and author profile page at https://www.totallybound.com

Home of Erotic Romance

Sign up for our newsletter and find out about all our romance book releases, eBook sales and promotions, sneak peeks and FREE romance books!